DIVIDED ROAD

THE ROAD TO ROCKTOBERFEST

ANNE BARWELL

ISBN: 978-1-99-116214-4 (epub)
ISBN: 978-1-99-116215-1 (print)

Grindstone belongs to Gabbi Grey.
The F-Holes belong to Ari McKay.
Both bands and their associated characters appear courtesy of their authors.

ISBN: 978-1-99-116214-4 (epub)
ISBN: 978-1-99-116215-1 (print)

To all the musicians I've played and worked with, and to the other Rocktoberfest authors. I've loved being able to play in this world.

ACKNOWLEDGMENTS

To Angela for beta reading, all her support, and the brilliant brainstorming conversations we've had.

To Janet for beta reading, and being a fabulous PA and cheerleader.

To Gabbi and Ari for inviting my guys and yours to meet at Rocktoberfest.

To my writing and reading communities for your support and friends, in particular RWNZ, and my Facebook group Anne's Books and Brews. A special thanks to the New Zealand Rainbow Romance Writers group—you guys rock.

Jo Clement from Covers by Jo for her wonderful cover art.

Penny for editing.

Lissa and Maryann for proofing.

To my family. Love you.

CHAPTER ONE

Owen ran his bow across the strings of his fiddle, playing the last lingering note in the song they'd just finished in a slow diminuendo to silence. Then he took a step back for Clay to do his spiel.

"Thanks for the wonderful warm welcome!" Clay grinned at their appreciative audience. "Nothing less than I'd expect from the punters here at The Taniwha!"

The crowd cheered, and the guy behind the bar whistled. The pub owner and Clay had a mutual friend who'd asked the band to play at short notice that night to cover a cancellation. Most of their gigs were of that ilk, but not all, and if filling in got them noticed, who cared? Flightless had a reputation for being easy to work with and inexpensive. At this point, their priority was getting themselves out there and in demand, and that part of the plan was working perfectly.

Slowly, but perfectly.

"We have a special treat for you tonight, but I'm sure you want to meet the band before we play our final song." Clay made a show of holding his hand to his ear. He had showmanship in spades. "What's that? I can't hear you!"

"Introduce the band," someone yelled from the back of the room.

The door to the pub opened, and Rachel, their manager, slipped in. She usually tried to attend all their gigs, but that evening something had come up at the last minute, and she wasn't sure she could make it.

Clay gave her a nod and then continued. "Please welcome the lovely Kaci on drums!"

Kaci performed a drum roll and grinned. The same guy who'd yelled before wolf-whistled. Rachel narrowed her eyes.

"None of that, unless you're prepared to do it for the whole band," Clay said. "We're equal opportunity here, and, besides, we don't want to piss Kaci off. We'd be lost without her keeping the beat." He paused for a moment, then continued. "To the right of me is Phil on guitar."

Phil strummed a chord and waved.

"And Tyler on bass." Tyler took a mock bow and added a flourish. The crowd laughed.

"Lincoln on keyboard." Clay turned to their keyboard player. "I've heard rumours this guy can play anything."

Lincoln rolled his eyes and played the opening to chopsticks.

"And to my left is Owen on fiddle." Clay pretended to ignore Lincoln and moved on. "Although," he lowered his voice, "he sings occasionally too, if you ask nicely."

Owen laughed. He loved seeing Clay work the crowd. "Only if you ask nicely, and aren't you forgetting someone?"

"Am I?" Clay looked puzzled. "Oh right! I'm Clay, lead vocalist, and together we're Flightless!" He glanced at Owen, confirming this was the night they'd finally be playing something that wasn't a cover.

"Go for it." Owen put his fiddle under his chin, ignoring his shaky hand.

What if the crowd hated his song?

No one outside the band had heard it before.

Oh well, nothing like jumping in the deep end.

"As I said, tonight we have a special treat for you." Clay didn't miss a beat. "Until now, Flightless has only played covers, but that's about to change. This next number is one of Owen's songs, and I tell you, he's seriously talented."

He turned to Kaci. "One. Two. Three. Four."

She tapped her stick on the drum, echoing the count. Tyler joined in on bass, and then they repeated the simple rhythm together.

Owen played a haunting melody on the fiddle, his instrument echoing through the pub.

"Somewhere, I lost you." Clay grabbed the mic and sang the opening lines. "Lost my heart and soul. Come find me, find me. I'm waiting here for you."

"I'm waiting here for you." Owen lowered his fiddle and joined Clay in harmony. "Lost in time. Waiting for you."

Phil stepped up to the mic, his guitar repeating the melody, then speeding up. The rest of the band joined in, a mix of vocal and instrumental harmony.

Owen lifted his fiddle again, adding a Celtic sound to the song, losing himself in the music.

"Lost you, never again. Got me forever, ooh." Clay's gravelly voice provided the perfect timbre for the lyrics, his tone softening with the final bars.

"Got me forever, ooh." Owen lowered his instrument, and sang the final line, repeating Clay's words like a distant echo, fading away to nothing.

He looked out at the audience, his heart racing when he was met by silence.

Fuck, they hated it.

One of the women closest to the stage stood up, tears in

her eyes, and started clapping. "Let's hear it for Flightless," she yelled. "You guys are going places!"

"Hell yeah," Rachel called out from the back.

The audience clapped, several rising to their feet.

Clay bowed and gestured for the rest of the band to follow. "Knew they'd love it," he whispered to Owen. "Brilliant, mate."

"Wouldn't be without all of you." Owen blushed and turned around to the friends who'd long been more like family. "Encore?"

Clay held up four fingers, signalling the song they'd play next. They'd figured out a code a couple of gigs in. Although they had a few covers prepared, Clay was great at reading the room and choosing their encore.

Tyler played the opening bars on his bass, a rock song that was a favourite with every audience they'd played for, and the crowd started singing along.

By the time they'd finished, Owen was riding the high of the combination of music and the vibe in the pub. He was always nervous before a gig, but once the music took over, he lost himself in the performance. Their band had been playing together for nearly ten years and knew each other's talent inside and out. Following each other on a tangent sounded seamless, like they'd rehearsed it that way.

Clay gave another bow, and the rest of the band followed his lead. "See you next time! We'll be playing at Hills on Courtenay on Friday night. Hope to see you there." He took off his guitar, put it on its stand, and walked over to meet some of the punters half way, soon falling into easy conversation.

"Any plans for the rest of the weekend?" Kaci came up behind Owen, startling him.

"I need to switch gears and practice for Monday's rehearsal, but apart from that, nothing." Owen unwound his bow and rubbed the excess rosin off his fiddle before stowing it safely in his case.

"Clay and I are taking a trip up the coast tomorrow if you want to join us." Kaci swung her arm over his shoulder. "You need some downtime, or you'll wear yourself out. I worry about you being pulled in two directions with the band and orchestra, especially when we have a gig on a concert weekend."

"I've been doing it for years, and I'm fine." Owen fingered the gold cross around his neck, a present from his grand-mother. "And as long as I have cover for the time off at work, I'm all good."

Kaci snorted. "You could delegate some of those staff rosters to Jesse, you know, instead of spending hours on them whenever you need to take leave. He's more than capable of taking up some of the slack, and you don't have to do all the paperwork for the place yourself."

"I don't mind." Owen managed a music shop, working at Arpeggios part-time when he started uni, and working his way up. "And I love the job. Seeing someone's eyes light up when I demonstrate the potential of an instrument they're thinking about buying always makes my day."

"That job was made for you," Kaci told him, glancing up when Clay approached. "Just don't burn yourself out, okay?"

"Hiya, how's my favourite girl and guy?" Clay gave Kaci a chaste kiss on her cheek. "Very appreciative audience today. We need to play more of your songs at our next gig, Owen. We've rehearsed them already, so they're all set to go. What do you say?"

"I guess." Owen chewed on his lower lip. "What if this was a fluke? We're getting a following. I don't want to screw that up for us."

Rachel butted into the conversation, her gaze lingering on Clay's casual arm around Kaci's waist, the three of them tight-knit and showing it. "That song wasn't a one-off. I caught the end of your last practice. I'm guessing that song not being a cover, it was another of yours?"

Owen frowned, trying to remember what they'd finished with the other night. "Yeah. *Sorted* is one of mine."

"The one you just heard is called *Lost*," Kaci shot Owen a grin.

"Can you include both of those in Friday's gig?" Rachel pulled out her phone and took notes. "I've got someone coming who asked if you had anything else. He loved tonight's performance. He's looking for bands for a festival he's organising in the Hawkes Bay early next year."

"Is he still here?" Owen scanned the pub, hoping to spot the guy she'd been talking to while he'd been packing up.

Rachel shook her head. "He had to be somewhere. Called into the pub to collect something he'd forgotten earlier, and stopped to listen. He loved what you each bring to the band, especially your fiddle, and the Celtic sound in that song."

"Flightless wouldn't work without *all* of us," Owen said firmly. His songs came to life once the band was together. Alone, they didn't have the same energy. "And some of the other stuff I've written aren't ballads like *Lost*. I like to change things up."

The band had an 80s/90s vibe, although they included a few heavier rock tunes occasionally too.

"Keeps things sounding fresh too." Rachel nodded her approval. "I'll touch base during the week and see how things are going. I won't be late for your next gig. Sorry about that today. I had a meeting that ran over."

"It's no problem," Clay reassured her. "She never seems to run out of energy," he added once Rachel left. "And I've never heard her say anything less than positive."

"Rachel?" Lincoln came up behind them. "Yeah, she's great." He'd connected her with the band, as she was a friend of a friend's. "Hey, I'm heading out, and might be late for practice on Friday."

"Do you want us to start later, and is everything okay?" Clay asked.

"Thanks, but no need. Mum's not been feeling well. I've talked her into seeing the doctor, and I'm going with her to make sure she doesn't downplay anything. You know how she is."

"Give her our love," Kaci said.

Lincoln's mum, Beth, had supported the band since they'd first started practising together in her garage while they were still in high school. She was the unofficial band 'aunty,' and they loved her dearly.

"I will," Lincoln promised. "Later!" He adjusted his satchel, his expression faltering before he turned away.

"He's worried," Owen said softly. "I hope Beth's okay." She was the only family Lincoln had left; they'd always been close.

"I'll check in with him tomorrow," Kaci promised. "Speaking of which, it's getting late, and I need my beauty sleep."

"Definitely." Phil laughed, and he and Tyler wandered over hand in hand. They'd been a couple for a few months after spending years being oblivious to their feelings for each other, although everyone else had seen their connection when they'd met.

Kaci poked out her tongue at him. "Despite your rude comment, I'm presuming you'd both still like a ride home?"

"You're not going to leave us to catch the bus?" Tyler sounded horrified, then he grinned. "But we've already loaded our instruments into your car."

"Arse," murmured Phil, kissing Tyler's cheek. "And, yes, we'd love a ride home if the offer's still there." He blinked his eyes at Kaci. "You still love us, right?"

7

"I'm thinking about it." Kaci laughed and then turned back to Owen and Clay.

The pub had settled into a murmur of conversation against the background of easy-listening music streaming from speakers on the walls. Most of the crowd had left apart from a couple of groups who'd settled in for late-night drinks in the hour or so before closing.

"See you tomorrow. I'll call you late morning when I'm on my way." Clay winked at Kaci. "Don't worry; I'll be sure to give you plenty of time for that beauty sleep you mentioned."

"See that you do." Kaci shuffled Tyler and Phil towards the door. They'd settle in and talk for hours, given the chance. Years later, they still all enjoyed each other's company, despite all the time they'd spent together.

"So, are you coming with us up the coast tomorrow?" Clay asked.

"I need to practice for Monday's rehearsal," Owen said cautiously. "And I don't want to interrupt anything."

Clay snorted. "As if. Kaci and I are friends, that's all, despite some fans thinking otherwise."

"One of Al's friends is convinced you're together, despite him swearing otherwise." Owen's brother loved music, enjoyed their gigs, but preferred to play classical. He was an accomplished flautist and music teacher, much to their parent's delight.

"I love Kaci, but like a sister." Clay shrugged. "Besides, I'm not her type, any more than she's yours."

Owen, Clay, and Kaci had started Flightless between them, with Lincoln joining them soon afterwards. They'd started rehearsing in the music rooms at their high school, and once they'd left school and realised they were good enough to play professionally, they advertised for guitar and bass players. Tyler and Phil had been the first to audition, and the band hadn't looked back.

"Do you need a ride home?" Owen deliberately didn't answer Clay's question about joining him and Kaci tomorrow.

"Nah, I've got my bike. Car's getting fixed. Again." Clay caught Owen's arm before he could make a clean getaway. "Take some time out, okay? Think about where you're going before you get to the crossroads? Something's gonna give with your workload, and I don't want it to be you."

"I'll try."

CHAPTER TWO

Saturday came around too quickly, and yet not fast enough. Owen's exhaustion lifted immediately when they began playing for the appreciative crowd. He loved performing with the orchestra, but those concerts didn't give him the same buzz.

After their first set, a dark-haired guy in his forties moved tables to sit with Rachel, and they began chatting in earnest.

Owen chugged water from his bottle. "Is that the guy Rachel was talking to at the Taniwha?" he whispered to Clay.

"Might be." Clay shrugged. "I didn't get a good look at him, but they both seem excited, so I'm hoping he is."

"If my songs don't put him off." Owen stowed his water bottle and picked up his violin. He loved the informal atmosphere of the pubs they played. Although he was still performing, the ambience felt more intimate, especially when the audience joined in some of the popular covers they played.

"Good thing I know you're not serious." Clay's expression told Owen he'd better not be.

"Umm, kind of. Maybe?" Owen ventured. If Kaci heard

him voice his doubts out loud, she'd kick his arse, and remind him seven ways to Sunday how good his songs were. At least he had one fan. Although the rest of the band, and Rachel, agreed with her.

Clay shook his head. "One day, you'll realise how much you rock."

"Yeah, whatever." No matter how well their gigs went, Owen's parents always congratulated him, then followed up with a reminder that they weren't a way to make a living and didn't have the same kudos that classical music did.

"Ready for round two?" Hills's manager, Ricky, asked. "Loved your first set. This place is buzzing tonight. I'll be talking to your manager about booking you in next month for another evening."

"Thanks," Clay said. "That would be great. We're loving being here."

"No point if you're not enjoying it too." Ricky stepped up to the microphone. "Please give Flightless another round of applause before they start their second set. Let's show them more of the hospitality we at Hills are known for!"

The audience clapped, and a couple at the back whistled loudly.

Clay didn't introduce *Lost* this time. Instead, he turned to Kaci, and she started the beat with her sticks before Tyler joined her on bass.

As soon as Clay started singing, the pub grew quiet, their focus shifting to Owen when he added his violin to the sound.

When the final notes died away, to be followed by thunderous applause, Clay tapped the microphone. "As you've probably guessed, that song wasn't a cover, but the second only performance of *Lost* by our own fiddle player, Owen." He gestured to Owen to take a bow. "Our lad's a bit on the shy side, but I think we should play another of his songs.

What do you think? Do you want to be the first to hear *Sorted*?"

"Hell yes!" A woman at the back yelled out. Someone laughed, and then everyone applauded.

"Guess we're doing it then," Clay told them. He turned to Kaci who led them into Owen's second song, *Sorted*.

Once Kaci and Phil on guitar played the first opening phrase, Owen stepped up to the microphone and echoed it on his fiddle, then added another phrase, and another. Clay hummed along softly, before taking up the melody.

"Thought my life was sorted until I met you."

"First time I saw you, I knew you were the one." Kaci's rich alto answered Clay. She usually didn't sing, although she had a fabulous voice.

Owen had written this one for her and for Clay. No doubt it would fuel the rumours they were together, but they sounded great, and neither of them cared what anyone thought.

"Now I'm looking back and wondering... I'm wondering." Clay turned to Kaci, both of them singing the next line together. "I want a future with you. Wishful thinking, or something real?"

They faded away to nothing, leaving Owen and Tyler to play together without guitar or drums, with Lincoln vamping on keyboard, highlighting the chord progressions alongside Tyler.

When they got to the chorus, several of the audience were tapping their feet along with the rhythm.

"Definitely something real," Kaci sang.

"Definitely something real," Clay agreed.

The rest of the band stopped playing, and Kaci and Clay repeated the last line a cappella, gradually slowing to the final note.

The audience stood and applauded.

"More!" someone called out.

"Okay." Owen shrugged. They had one more original song they hadn't played yet. Shit, if that went down well too, he'd have another kind of problem. He'd need to write more.

Hopefully, one of the other band members would cave and work with him. He loved composing but was already stretched thin, time-wise.

"This one's called *Patterns in the Sand*, and it's more of a ballad than the last two." Clay stepped away from the microphone, and Owen moved closer.

He licked his dry lips before speaking. "Thanks for your appreciation." Owen cleared his throat and focused on Rachel and the guy next to her, blocking out the rest of the room to curb his nervousness. "I hope you enjoy this song as much as the last two."

He played a C on his fiddle and then began to sing at the same pitch. "Tiny grains of sand reflecting the patterns in my heart. Changing, lonely, needing more."

Lincoln joined him on keyboard, playing a harmony under Owen's solo.

"Torn between the shore and sea, drawn away, yearning to be free." Owen's voice steadied as he grew more confident.

"A lighthouse shines, beckoning those who dare." Clay sang the next line, pitching his voice lower, and keeping that melody as Owen repeated the words in harmony.

"I see the light, hope in the darkness. A haven I want to believe in." Owen picked up his fiddle and played a haunting melody in a minor key, continuing for several bars, with only Lincoln accompanying him.

"Find your pattern in the sand. Grab your future and hold on tight." Clay and Owen sang the chorus together, Tyler and Phil joining in for the rest of the song.

"Grabbing hold of you. Stay with me," Owen sang.

"I'll stay with you. I'm not letting go," Clay replied.

"Not letting go."

Phil picked out the fiddle's original melody on his guitar, but this time in a major key, finishing the song on a hopeful note.

When the music died away, a couple of people in the audience were sniffling. "Wow," a woman whispered to her companion. "That was beautiful."

"Where are you playing next?" someone called out. "Where can we find your songs?"

"Playing here again next month," Clay confirmed. "We'll leave some flyers here. Check out our social media, and don't forget to subscribe for updates. Thanks for being such a great audience."

He turned to Phil, signalling him to play the opening bar of an upbeat cover they often finished with.

When they'd finished, a couple of women approached the stage area. "Great music," one of them said. "Can I get your autograph? You'll be famous one day, and I'll be able to brag that I heard those songs first."

Clay laughed. "Of course."

She held out one of the flyers advertising that night's performance, and he signed it, each of the band adding their signatures.

Her companion smiled shyly. "I think it's so cool having a fiddle player with the band. Have you always played this kind of music?"

"I play in an orchestra, too." Owen signed her flyer too, grinning at her surprised expression. "Lincoln's also classically trained. You should hear his Chopin. It's sublime." He handed the second flyer around to the rest of the band.

"Wow, and thanks, and for a fabulous night too. I'll definitely be here when you play again. Bye for now."

"You've got yourself a fan there," Kaci said after the women left.

"*We've* got fans," Owen corrected.

"Well done. I knew the audience would love your songs." Rachel came over, the guy she'd been talking to close behind. "This is Duncan Fray. His family owns Frays Vineyard in the Hawkes Bay."

"Fray as in Frays Days?" Clay asked. "I've been to a few of your music festivals. They're great."

"Thanks." Duncan held out his hand and shook theirs in turn. "Rachel has been telling me about your band. I love that you've been playing together for so long, and I loved your performance tonight. I think your band would be a great fit for next year's festival."

"You want us to perform at the festival?" Kaci sounded excited. "Wow. That's awesome."

"Rachel and I need to work out some of the details, but I wanted to ask you in person, rather than through her." Duncan grinned. "I'm only in Wellington for a few more days, and I'm catching up with an old family friend later tonight so I need to get going. I'm looking forward to hearing from Rachel on your behalf. We also discussed a few other ideas, but I'll leave her to talk to you about those."

"It was great meeting up with you, Duncan," Rachel said. "I'll be in touch before you head back to the Bay so we have time to sort out some of the details." She paused. "Of course, the decision to play is up to the band. I'm merely their manager and chief herder."

"Like cats?" Duncan chuckled, his eyes twinkling. Owen liked him already. "Good luck with that. We have a few of those at the vineyard. You have my card. Phone me when you've made a decision. I'd love to get the contract signed by Tuesday if you're going ahead. The festival's popular and we like to confirm our lineup as far ahead as possible."

Clay met the gaze of each of the band in turn, and one by

one, they nodded. "We'll do it. This is too good an opportunity to turn down. Thank you."

"Great to hear it." Duncan zipped up his jacket. "I'll look forward to your call, and to hearing Flightless at the festival. Have a good evening. Bye."

"Wow," Kaci said. "I can't believe it. Flightless at Frays Days. We're going places!"

"Speaking of which," Rachel added. "As we need to travel from Wellington to the Hawkes Bay, Duncan and I were discussing a few extra performances along the way. He has a few connections at pubs scattered throughout the North Island. How do you feel about a road trip? We could hire a van and make a thing of it."

"Not too many stops, though, yeah?" Tyler said. "We don't want to screw up at the festival because we're too tired."

"Of course not." Rachel looked indignant that he'd thought she hadn't considered it. "Who's in? And if you want to think about it, that's fine too."

"Nothing to think about." Clay raised his hand, Kaci quickly following, as did Phil and Tyler.

Lincoln hesitated, then raised his hand.

Owen took a moment to think through his schedule. Frays Days was in March, and the orchestra's next concert was in May. He was owed time off work, so fitting in both felt very doable. "What about Bach?" He couldn't leave his cat. "Al can't take her. He has a dog, and my parents…." His parents would take the passive-aggressive route.

"Mum would love to take her for a while," Lincoln offered. "She and Bach have a mutual love thing going on, and she misses having a cat."

"Thanks." Owen raised his hand. "Looks like we're playing at Frays Days in March."

"You're not helping." Owen lifted his cat, Bach, off the piano and closed the lid. The few ideas he'd had for new songs weren't gelling,

He yawned and absently stroked Bach's fur when she immediately settled on his lap. Hopefully, the words would flow better when he wasn't so tired. He never had any problems finding melodies, but lyrics were another matter. Refining his rough outlines so they didn't suck arse was only fueling his frustration.

Frays Days wasn't until late March. They had three months yet. Owen sighed and tried not to think about how he'd lost one month already since Rachel had finalised their agreement with Duncan Fray. Composing under pressure never worked well. He'd ignore his attempts at composing for Christmas week and get back to it in the New Year.

Christmas wasn't something he looked forward to, with his parents already reminding him of his obligation to visit over the holidays. He'd much prefer to sit on his back porch with a few beers and soak up the sun.

He loved his parents and enjoyed spending time with Al and his family. Owen doted on his nephews, but he didn't need a couple of days of his parents reminding him he needed to focus more on his classical career rather than the choices he'd made that, in their eyes, were a waste of time, and had no future.

Wait until they found out the band was playing at Frays.

Maybe, a hopeful inner voice whispered, *they'd be proud of him and wish him well.*

Yeah, nah. If he was in luck, they'd voice the words, but wouldn't be able to hide the disappointment lacing their tone.

Owen flicked the switch on the kettle and spooned some tea into a pot. He had scones in the freezer somewhere, courtesy of Aunt Dawn. He fossicked around while the kettle boiled and threw them into the microwave to defrost.

He'd just poured his tea, and was spreading jam on his scones when the doorbell rang.

Bach pricked up her ears and meowed. She tilted her head sideways, jumped onto the floor and smooched around his legs.

"You're not getting these scones," Owen told her, shoving his plate into the pantry. She loved anything baked and always hung around looking hopeful whenever he pulled out a treat from the cupboard or freezer.

"Coming," he called in the direction of the doorway. Who'd call on him on a Monday afternoon? He'd swapped shifts with Jesse and worked Saturday, so he would usually be at work now.

Lincoln stood at the doorway. He was wet through, water from his hair dripping in splotches down his thin jacket. "Hope I'm not disturbing you. I went to Arpeggios, and they said you had the day off, so I figured I'd see if you were home."

"Did you walk?" Owen frowned. "I'll grab a towel, and I've just made some tea." He hadn't noticed it was raining, although he vaguely remembered hearing thunder in the distance some time before. "If you'd rung, I could have picked you up."

"It was fine when I left home, and I felt like walking." Lincoln didn't live far from the centre of Upper Hutt where Arpeggios was, although Owen's house was a good hour's walk further out in Heretaunga.

"Come in." Owen ushered Lincoln inside.

Something was definitely up. Lincoln never turned up unannounced, and his voice sounded choked like he'd been crying or coming down with a cold.

"Thanks." Lincoln bent to pet Bach, and then picked her

up, burying his face in her grey fur. She'd loved Lincoln the first time they'd met, shortly after Owen had adopted her as a kitten.

She licked rain droplets from his face and chattered to him in cat language. For some reason, she was always more vocal around Lincoln, while she only meowed at Owen when he'd shirked his duties and failed to top up her biscuits.

Owen grabbed a towel from the linen cupboard in the hallway. "Give me your jacket, and I'll hang it up in the laundry. I'll be in the kitchen when you're ready."

"I'm sorry to barge in on you, but I needed to talk, and you've always been good at listening." Lincoln gently put Bach down and handed Owen his jacket.

"I'm always here for you." Owen squeezed Lincoln's shoulder. He and Lincoln had always confided in each other first before sharing their troubles with the rest of the band. Clay was always supportive, but could be a little full-on at times. Tyler and Phil had headed north to Phil's family for the break, and Kaci was up the coast visiting her sister.

"I know, and I appreciate that." Lincoln managed a shaky smile. "Is that your aunt's scones I can smell?"

"Yeah. I'll pull out a few extra for you. I have a freezer full of the things." Owen wasn't surprised when Bach stayed with Lincoln, rubbing around his legs. She'd need towelling down too if she kept that up. "Do you need me to grab you a pair of shorts and a t-shirt?"

"Yeah, thanks." Lincoln bent to unlace his sneakers.

"Socks?"

"Nah, they're dry."

Owen disappeared into his room to get Lincoln dry clothes. Luckily, they were of a similar size. "I'll leave them in the bathroom for you. Throw your wet clothes over the side of the bath. If they're not dry by the time you leave, you can collect them next time." He deliberately didn't look back to see Lincoln's expression. The guy was upset. That much was obvious.

Ten minutes later, a much more composed Lincoln wandered into the kitchen. Owen placed a cup of tea in front of him, and a plate of scones between them. "What's up?"

"It's Mum." Lincoln slowly sipped his tea. "You know how I convinced her to go to the doctor's a few weeks back? Just before we played at Hills?"

"Yeah." A cold shiver ran through Owen, but he waited for Lincoln to tell him.

"We've been waiting on a few tests, and a scan." Lincoln bit his lip, his eyes filling with tears. "She didn't want me to say anything in case it was nothing. Damn it! I knew it wasn't nothing, but you know how stubborn she can be."

"Tenacious." Owen used the word Beth preferred. "That trait has seen you both through some hard times after your dad…." He trailed off.

"Died?" Lincoln bent down to pull Bach into his arms when she rubbed against his legs. "I can't lose her too. Not yet. It's too soon." He rubbed at his eyes, accepting the box of tissues Owen handed him. "She has cancer. An aggressive one. God knows how long it's been growing inside her. She's going to need surgery and chemo and…."

"You need to be there for her." Owen guessed what was coming. "Sounds like she has a few rough months ahead." He had to believe Beth would pull through, and not just for Lincoln's sake.

"Yeah." Lincoln grew quiet again. He nibbled on the edge of a scone instead of demolishing it like he usually did. "I can't play with you in March. I need to be with Mum. I'd never forgive myself if I wasn't there for her. If I don't have her for much longer, I want to make memories with her and take care of her like she's always done for me. You understand that, don't you?"

Owen couldn't promise everything would be okay. "Whatever you need, we'll support you." Shit, where were they going to find another keyboard player as talented as Lincoln. "Do you want me to tell the rest of the band?"

"I was hoping we could do it together." Lincoln looked hopeful, and then relieved when Owen nodded.

"Of course." Owen glanced up at the calendar. "We're two days out from Christmas, and everyone's away, except for Clay. Better that we tell them at the same time so you don't have to go through it twice, yeah?"

"And Rachel." Lincoln looked glum. "I'm letting you down. We finally get a big break, and I'm ditching you."

"You're *not* ditching us!" Owen slid off his chair and walked around the breakfast bar to pull Lincoln into a hug. "Your priority is your mum. You'd never forgive yourself if you weren't there for her, supporting her through this. Even if she's okay by the time we leave for Frays, there are all the rehearsals leading up to the performance. You don't need that pressure on top of everything else."

Lincoln rested his head on Owen's shoulder, his body shaking with emotion. He'd always appreciated hugs and was a good guy who deserved more than this shitty mess life had thrown his way. He'd broken up with his last partner a few months back, so he had no one to call on.

"Thank you," he whispered. "You give the best hugs."

"Don't let your mum hear you say that."

"I'm going to miss her so much."

"Hey, she's not gone yet. She's a fighter, and so are you. Cancer is not always a death sentence. When does she start treatment?"

"In the new year." Lincoln let out a long sigh. "I was excited to be playing at Frays. It's like a dream come true."

"If we're a hit, perhaps they'll invite us back next year?" Owen caught Lincoln's gaze. "We'll need another keyboard player to fill in for you, but that's all they'll be. A fill-in. You're as much a part of Flightless as all of us. We've built up this band together. Whoever we get, we'll clarify that it's only for…. How long do you need?"

"Six months at least, maybe a year?" Lincoln wiped his nose. "If…" He faltered. "If something happens, I'm going to need some time to sort things out and figure out my future."

"Do you need any financial help?"

"Mum's got insurance, and it's more than enough for treatment and to cover her expenses for the next year. I'm already working remotely and only going into the office once a week. They're happy for me to do that less often if I need to. I also have a stash of leave if I need it." Lincoln worked as a software engineer for one of the leading New Zealand banks.

"If you need one of us to sit with her when you have to go in, please ask?" Owen hesitated. "Is it okay if I tell Aunt Dawn? She'd be happy to spend some time with Beth and give you a break too, and she's only working four days a week now."

"Thanks. I'll talk to her after we see the band. I'm sure Mum would like that though. They've always got on well." Lincoln rolled his eyes. "A little too well, truth be told."

"Yeah, I'm sure they'll be plotting together in no time." Owen was pleased to see Lincoln perk up a little.

"I'm going to miss playing with you guys." Lincoln finished his tea and reached for another scone.

"You need a break and we're not going anywhere."

"Yeah, but you only need one keyboard player." Lincoln ruffled Bach's fur.

"Come round here and jam anytime," Owen offered. He'd always enjoyed playing with Lincoln, and their music always distracted him from anything troubling him. "You will need to take some breaks, or you'll get burnt out."

"I'd like that." Lincoln chewed thoughtfully. "I might know a guy who could step in and play for you. He's between bands at present. Want me to talk to him?"

"Sure." Owen wasn't looking forward to finding someone to fill their gap. "Anyone with the Lincoln seal of approval is more than welcome to audition."

"Hopefully, he'll be a good fit, and you won't need to look any further." Lincoln scratched at the back of his head. "I'd offer to help with the auditions, but I'm not sure I could cope with that to be honest." He grimaced.

"As I said, they're filling in, *not* replacing you."

"Hope not." Lincoln shook his head when Owen opened his mouth to protest. "Let's cross that road when we get to it. One step at a time." He stood. "I should get going. The rain's stopped, so at least I won't drown getting home."

"Do you want a lift?"

"I think better when I walk, and I need to do quite a bit of that at present." Lincoln gave Owen one last hug. "I'll collect my clothes later unless you want to throw them in a bag for me?"

"Later is fine. Keep in touch, okay?" Owen followed Lincoln to the front door. "And maybe talk to the keyboard guy in the new year once we've talked to the band?" Any decision they made needed to be a joint one, including finding Lincoln's *temporary* replacement.

"Yeah, of course." Lincoln laced up his sneakers. "I've known him a while. I think you'd like him."

Owen raised an eyebrow. "Even now, you just can't help yourself, can you?" He was still recovering from his last very messy breakup. Two years ago felt like yesterday in many ways and he wasn't in a hurry to go through that again.

"Not everyone's like Deb. Brent and I still keep in touch."

"My breakup with Mike wasn't any easier." Owen didn't do relationships well, with Mike and Deb the last in a string of exes to show for it. Kaci's theory was that Owen couldn't shake off an encounter at a party years ago, and no one he'd been with since matched up to a dream guy who'd vanished afterwards.

"Ending a relationship isn't easy unless you weren't that invested in the first place." Lincoln paused in the doorway. "If you need someone to talk to while you're recovering from Christmas, you know where to find me."

"Thanks." Owen wouldn't burden Lincoln with that this year. He had enough on his plate. "Take care, okay?"

Lincoln answered with a nod, instead of his usual "always," and took off down the road.

Owen stood in the doorway, watching until Lincoln reached the end of the street.

CHAPTER THREE

"You want me to audition for Flightless? Seriously?" Jared's hand shook. He lowered his coffee cup carefully, not wanting to smash the thing. His sister, who owned the café where he regularly met up with Lincoln, would not be impressed.

A mix of excitement and terror raced through him, the former finally winning out.

"I wouldn't have asked you otherwise."

"But you're their keyboard player." Jared narrowed his eyes. "You love playing for them, and you guys are finally getting noticed. It's not a good time to take a break."

He and Lincoln hadn't seen each other for a few months, life getting in the way. They'd studied music together at Victoria University, and kept in touch. Lincoln was living the dream playing in a band, while each time Jared thought he'd found his forever band, they broke up.

"And besides," he continued, "given my track record, I don't want to be the guy who broke up Flightless."

Lincoln snorted. "You didn't break up those bands. If anything, you held them together for months longer than they should have lasted. It's not your fault you end up working with musicians who think way too highly of them-selves. Clash of the Bands, my arse. More like Clash of the Egos for that last band you were with." He sobered and broke his scone into bits. "Mum's sick. I need to stay with her."

"Oh, shit. I'm sorry." Jared reached across the table and squeezed Lincoln's hand. He'd only met Beth a few times, but she'd always made him feel welcome. Given Lincoln's demeanour, whatever was wrong must be serious. "And sure, anything I can do to help, ask."

"I'm asking you to audition for Flightless," Lincoln said evenly. "I feel bad that I'm deserting them, especially as they've been supportive as hell. You'd be a good fit, and you're talented. They're playing Frays Days in March, and you'd have no trouble picking up the music."

"Frays Days? Shit." Jared had dreamed of playing there since his parents had taken him and Brigit to one of the festivals when they were kids. "I can stay with Beth if you want to play."

Lincoln shook his head. "I appreciate the offer, but there are the rehearsals leading up and everything else that goes with that. I'm not in the right headspace." He bit his lip, anguish in his eyes, although he almost managed to hide it. "Thing is, I might come back to the band after... I'm not thinking that far ahead yet. If you joined them, would you be okay with it being temporary?"

"Sure." Jared didn't hesitate. "This is a huge opportunity, if they'll have me, but not at the cost of shoving you out. I've dreamed of being part of a decent band, even for a while, and Frays is the icing on the cake."

"Thanks." Lincoln pulled out his phone and sent a text. "I've sent you Owen's details. He's expecting your call. I didn't mention you by name, in case you didn't want to, so you'll have to introduce yourself. Tell him you're Lincoln's keyboard guy."

"I can do that." Jared stood after Lincoln did. He pulled Lincoln into a hug. Beth's illness must be really bad for Lincoln to ditch the band when they were preparing to play at Frays. "I meant what I said about helping if you need it."

"Thanks." Lincoln sounded choked. "I'll call you." He gave Brigit a wave and left before she could talk to him.

"He left more than he ate." Brigit slid into the chair Lincoln had vacated. "Not like him at all. What's up?"

Jared quickly filled her in.

"Shit, poor guy." Brigit looked thoughtful. "I'll bake some of his favourites and send a care package to him, and another for Beth." She adjusted the tea towel over her shoulder. "So, you're playing with Flightless, hmm? Go you."

"They haven't heard me yet." Jared wasn't about to presume anything. He'd been turned down by more bands than he cared to remember. Lincoln might think he'd be a good fit, but he hadn't heard him play for a while. He was out of practice, and nowhere as good as Lincoln.

Brigit narrowed her eyes in the 'I'm not taking any of your shit' look he knew all too well. "You're a talented musician, and those other bands were shite. They probably turned you down so you wouldn't show them up."

"You're my sister. Of course, you'd say that," Jared murmured.

"When have I not been completely honest with you?" Brigit glanced up at the sound of the counter bell. "Julie's got a queue, but don't think this conversation is over, 'cause it's not."

"Yes, Mum." Jared couldn't help but smile at the familiarity of her response.

He and Brigit were close, even more so since their parents had died in a car accident ten years before. They were only a year apart in age, so they had pretty much raised each other. Although Brigit ran The Strawberry Scone, she and Jared had bought it between them with part of their inheritance. He'd taken a correspondence course in accountancy and a barista course at Polytech after he'd finished his degree, although these days, he preferred to pick up casual work in various pubs around the area, occasionally filling in for Brigit. He'd hoped to one day be in a successful band and supplement his income with his bar work and his share of the profits from the café.

Hopefully, Flightless could be the stepping stone to that, although it would only be temporary.

But someone noticing him would be all he needed.

Jared grinned. Finally!

Then he sighed, feeling like an arse. He'd lost his parents and wouldn't wish that on anyone. He hoped this opportunity hadn't come at the price of Lincoln's heartache.

∼

Jared checked the address against the GPS on his phone. He was in the right place, but the house in front of him looked too small to host regular band rehearsals. Maybe it belonged to one of the band members, and they practised in the living room?

Some of the other places he'd rehearsed in hadn't been great. He couldn't wait to get out of some of the damp and dimly lit places. There'd definitely been a weird smell coming from the corner of the garage where the last band he'd been with practised. He'd cut his losses and run from those guys. They'd been weird, and the sickly whiff of pot had put him right off.

Shame they hadn't meshed, or so he'd told them. He doubted they noticed he left because they were so stoned.

Lincoln had told him not to worry about bringing a keyboard. He'd left his spare with the band.

Jared climbed the steps to the front door and knocked. Owen had sounded friendly when they'd spoken on the phone, despite the awkward situation. Jared had been to a few of their gigs, but never met any of them, although he'd bumped into Owen at a party years ago. He and Lincoln tended to move in different circles.

He remembered Owen being hot, but Jared had been younger and less sure of himself back then. An attempt to introduce himself had soon digressed into him spilling beer down himself and Owen, and backing away quickly while mumbling an embarrassed apology.

Hopefully, that night had disappeared into the recesses of Owen's memory, never to surface again.

Music sounded faintly in the distance, tugging at Jared's soul. A lone violin weaved a melancholy melody above a bass and guitar.

Wow. Jared swallowed, his palms sweaty, his nervousness growing ten-fold. He yearned to be a part of the music, adding his keyboard to the mix. A man began to sing, his voice low at first, then building in volume.

Finally, the music stopped. Jared knocked again, spotted the doorbell and rang it, the sound reverberating in the early evening air.

A few moments later, the front door swung open. Owen Stanton was everything Jared remembered from that party and more. He'd filled out and wore his hair longer, wisps of light brown hanging over his forehead. He wore jeans, a black t-shirt and hoodie.

"I'm Jared Murphy. We spoke on the phone."

"Lincoln's friend, yeah." Owen broke into a grin. "He didn't tell me you were Beer Guy."

"Beer Guy?" Jared's heart sank. *Oh fuck, Owen did recognise him.*

"You were at one of Lincoln's parties about ten years ago?

You spilt beer down yourself, and me?" Owen seemed amused rather than annoyed. "I usually don't forget a face, and you're... rather unforgettable."

"I'm sorry." Jared wasn't sure what else to say.

A short blonde woman appeared behind Owen. "Don't be an arse," she said. "We don't leave visitors on the doorstep."

Owen mumbled something and took a step back. "Sorry, I didn't mean to be rude. I just... wasn't expecting...."

"Me?" Jared said, helpfully.

"Jared, right? I'm Kaci, and this is Owen." Kaci gestured inside. "Come on in and meet the rest of the band. Lincoln has been singing your praises. We're looking forward to jamming with you."

"Nice to meet you." Jared avoided Owen's stare. Did he have something on his T-shirt? "Looks like Owen and I briefly met years ago."

Kaci giggled. "Yeah, I heard enough of your conversation to figure that out." She looked him up and down, her dark eyes full of amusement. "So, *you're* the one who got away that night, hmm?"

"Kaci!" Owen looked mortified. "I told you that in confidence."

"Moving on." Kaci gave Jared a wink. "Sorry." She linked her arm through his and led him down a hallway that opened into an enormous room. "This used to be the garage, but Rachel had it converted into a studio for us. Renting space is expensive, and she wasn't using it anyway."

"Wow. It's... impressive." And not what Jared was expecting from the street.

The room looked to have been a double garage, with the roller door at the far end, the band with their instruments in the middle, and a sofa on the other wall. A sink, fridge, and bench ran down the wall to the left of the door they'd walked through.

"Good space, eh?" A tall, well-built man with a shock of red hair approached them and held out his hand. "I'm Clayton Tulloch, but my friends call me Clay." He shook hands. "Nice to meet you." Clay indicated the remaining band members. "That's Tyler Hollister on bass, and Phil Brindle on guitar."

"And I'm Rachel Irving." A woman not much older than Lincoln walked up behind them. "I manage this lot, or attempt to." She chuckled. "I hope you'll be joining us while Lincoln's away."

"You haven't heard me play yet," Jared protested.

"We're about to." Rachel smiled, her eyes twinkling. "Can I grab you something to drink? We have tea, coffee, and juice."

Jared was pleased nothing stronger was on offer before a rehearsal, though he was looking forward to a beer afterwards. "I've brought my water bottle, but I'd love some tea later." He looked apologetic. "I don't drink coffee, sorry."

"A man after my own heart." Rachel sounded smug. "I keep telling these guys that the world doesn't run on coffee and that some of us can work well without a direct infusion of it."

"Whatever," chorused Owen and Clay, like a well-rehearsed routine.

"Keyboard's over here." Phil rolled his eyes in clear amusement. "Are you familiar with our songs?"

"He's not going to audition otherwise, right?" Tyler gave Phil a long-suffering look. "Don't mind him. He thinks he's funny."

"But you still love me anyway." Phil looked sad.

"Of course." Tyler gave him a quick peck on the cheek, definitely not one like you'd give a friend.

So, they're together. Lincoln hadn't given Jared any clues about the band dynamics and teased that he'd soon work it out.

He'd heard rumours that Clay and Kaci were a couple, but so far he had seen no sign of it, although they were very touchy-feely around each other. Owen had kept out of the media as much as was possible, but damn, he looked good in a suit in his classical violinist role.

Although Jared much preferred the relaxed, casual version of Owen now. He felt real, whereas the other gave a persona vibe. The guy definitely had mad skills in both classical and rock.

"And?" Clay asked.

"Hmm, what?" Jared realised everyone was waiting for him to speak. What was the question again? Oh yeah. "I love your music, with its rock slash Celtic vibe." He'd played along to a few of their songs to get a feel for them. Lincoln was right. Jared did fit. With the music, at least.

"Right answer." Clay grinned. "We'll start with some covers, well-known songs that you'll already be familiar with, and then move on to the originals. Owen's got a new one we were going to try today if you're up for it."

"Totally." Jared played a couple of scales, and then a few arpeggios to get the feel of the keyboard. It was a good one, almost up to the standard of the one he had at home.

"So you and Lincoln went to Vic together?" Owen asked. "Music major?"

"I double majored in that and English Lit," Jared confirmed. Both were subjects with limited job opportunities, but he wanted to pursue his passions.

"Nice one." Owen grinned. "Music for me, though I snuck in a few history papers on the side."

"You'll have to compare notes." Kaci grinned.

Owen narrowed his eyes. Her grin widened.

"When you're ready," Clay said.

He, Kaci, and Owen seemed tight. Phil and Tyler weren't as vocal but seemed amused by the banter. Jared relaxed. Already, this didn't feel like other auditions he'd been to.

"What are we starting with?" Jared asked.

"You know, *Take Me*?" Clay referred to a song made popular by a Kiwi band a few years ago.

Jared nodded. He'd played the song with other bands. He could do this.

Kaci counted them in, and then Phil joined on bass. Jared saw his opening, mirrored the bass line, and then added a discreet counter melody over basic chords.

Owen raised his fiddle, and to Jared's surprise, followed his lead.

When the song was finished, Clay led them into a song by a different band, and then another in a completely different style. After a few, he stopped and chugged water, giving Jared a thumbs up.

Jared reached for his water bottle and drank heavily. His throat was dry, although he hadn't sung.

"I love what you did in that last song," Rachel said. "Not quite Lincoln, but not so different that it changes the feel of it."

"I'm not Lincoln, and I'm not here to replace him." Jared wanted that made clear right from the beginning.

Clay held up his hand. "Yeah, we got that memo from Owen, too. No worries. We're glad to have you, and appreciate you stepping into the breach at short notice."

Jared swallowed. Did that mean they wanted him? "Umm, okay...."

"Of course, any decision will be made by everyone. We're a democratic lot here, but so far, I'm impressed." Clay glanced around the room, and to Jared's relief, everyone gave him a thumbs up. "You've demonstrated that you're great at covers, but what about original songs? Owen's have a different feel to them, more Celtic than rock, and he has a couple of ballads in the mix too."

"I haven't heard any of them yet." Jared hadn't been able to find any of them to listen to on Flightless' social media or streaming accounts. The songs were too new, and Lincoln had warned him that might be the case. They planned to put some out there in a few weeks to start the hype for their performance at Frays.

"I have music," Owen offered, "or you can follow my lead. How's your ear?"

"Pretty good. I'm comfortable with either sight reading or playing by ear."

"Great." Owen put down his water bottle and picked up his violin. "I'd love to see what you do with this one. We've only played it in public once at Hills in December, and I've made a few tweaks since then."

"Okay."

Owen played a C on his violin and then began to sing. The words and melody were beautiful, his clear tenor rising above the guitar when Phil joined in.

Caught up in the music, Jared hummed along with the harmony he added underneath, his voice merging with Owen's, then breaking away. After a few moments, he stopped, realising that everyone else had stopped playing.

He flushed, heat spreading through him. "Shit, sorry. I didn't intend to do that and barge into your solo. I won't do it again."

"Lincoln didn't say you could sing," Owen said slowly.

"I don't, usually." Jared had a passable voice and could hold a melody, but mainly only sang in the shower. However, something about being with the band had shaken off his inhibitions, and he'd joined in like he and Owen had sung together forever.

Owen and Clay exchanged a look before Clay spoke.

"Your voice is great and added to the song. If you want to sing again, you should. We'll tell you if it's not working, but I think it will."

"*Patterns in the Sand* is a love song." Owen hesitated. "I wrote it, thinking of two guys. Clay's our lead singer, but not the timbre I heard in my head. Yours is."

"I don't want…." Bad enough that Jared was taking Lincoln's spot. He didn't want to get too comfortable and encroach on anyone else's role.

"We've all sung on different songs," Clay reassured him. "I'm happy to step back and support you and Owen in this one. If you want to, of course. Singing in public is way different to doing it here."

"I'd like to, if that's okay," Jared said shyly. He'd never been asked to do anything like this before. "I'll give it a go at least."

"Right, that's sorted then." Rachel sounded delighted. "I think you're going to be a great fit, Jared. Welcome to Flightless."

"Thanks. I won't let you down." Jared's hands shook. Fuck, he'd never been complimented like that before, or made to feel so welcome.

CHAPTER FOUR

Owen finger combed his hair again, but the errant curl sticking up at angles refused to lie flat. He sighed and glanced in the mirror in a last-ditch effort to reassure himself that it didn't look that bad.

He was being ridiculous. Jared was coming around to try out some new harmonies for some of Owen's songs. This wasn't a date, and besides, as he'd reminded Lincoln, Owen wasn't looking to date again.

Not for a long time, if ever.

Jared being hot didn't factor in. Owen's last two dating attempts had been gorgeous, yet their looks hadn't been enough to save their relationships.

Dark hair, pale skin, and green eyes. Jared had filled out since that party all those years ago and was no longer a skinny high school kid. He'd put on muscle and height, now standing a fraction taller than Owen.

Deb and Mike both had dark hair and light-coloured eyes. Blue, though, not green.

A coincidence. Totally.

He walked out to the kitchen, checking that the scones

he'd scrounged off Brigit at the Strawberry Scone were still fresh and that he had plenty of milk for tea. Or coffee.

The coffee machine spluttered, reminding Owen that Jared didn't drink coffee.

Fuck, he was losing it.

They were getting together to make music.

"Bach," he called, retrieving the cat's biscuit container from the pantry and shaking it. "Food time!" Better to get feeding her out of the way before Jared arrived, although Bach wasn't shy in reminding anyone that it was her dinner time.

Owen shook the container again. Where the hell was she? She couldn't have gone far. Despite her being an indoor cat, his house was big enough for her to roam and find hiding places. Frowning, he checked her regular spots, but couldn't find her.

His heart started to race. Surely, she had to be somewhere. He sprinted into the laundry, his heart sinking at the half-open window over the washing machine. He'd shut that and fastened the lock. He knew he had.

"Bach! Here, girl, here kitty." Owen leaned over the washing machine, and pulled at the window fastening, slamming it shut. He pushed at it, and it opened again. Damn it. He'd have to replace it. That must have been how she'd escaped.

The doorbell sounded. Owen strode to the front door, hoping to see someone holding his errant cat.

Instead, Jared stood there. "What's up?" he said immediately.

"My cat's escaped." Owen filled him in quickly. "Sorry, I need to look for her first. She's not used to being outside, and hasn't enough sense to stay off the road."

A huge truck rumbled past. A chill went up Owen's spine. What if he was already too late?

"You've checked the house?" Jared stated the obvious.

"First thing I did." Owen stepped to one side to let Jared in.

"I'll help you look." Jared dumped his backpack under the coat rack. "If we split up, we might find her sooner. Is there a window she loves looking out of? Perhaps her dash for freedom has led her there?"

"I think she got out the laundry window." Owen led Jared out the front door and round the side of the house. "The catch needs fixing, or so I just found out. She's pushed it open."

"Duct tape will fix it until you get it changed." Jared strode over to the window, pulled it open as far as it would go, and then peered inside. "Owen, what does your cat look like?"

"Bach's a grey tabby." Owen held out his hands to show her size by the distance between them. "About this big. She's a friendly thing, loves everyone, and shows it by shedding over them."

"And also has a fondness for laundry?" Jared glanced at Owen, his mouth turning up in amusement. "Come look at this. I can see a grey tabby tail sticking out of your laundry basket. If that's your cat, she's buried herself in a pile of towels."

"Bloody cat." Owen got up on his toes so he could look inside. Immediately, a familiar furry head poked out over the basket and made a meowy sound, the one that usually meant she wasn't impressed he'd disturbed her. "I swear she wasn't in there before."

"Perhaps she was outside and jumped back in while you were looking for her?" Jared ran his fingers over the edge of the window, wiping off a good amount of fur. "There's a build-up on the wood. She might have been doing this for a while."

Owen narrowed his eyes. "Bloody cat," he repeated. "God, sorry, I feel like an idiot now. Come in and I'll find some tape for the window, and make you a cuppa."

"Don't. Feel like an idiot, that is." Jared pushed the window shut. "My sister has a tabby, and we spent a couple of hours last summer looking for him, only to find that he'd discovered a comfy spot in her hot water cupboard and settled in for a nap."

"I have an outside tank, or I'm sure Bach would have tried that already." Owen stepped back to get out of Jared's way. "She loves laundry."

"So does Dolce." Jared grinned and followed Owen around the house to the front door.

"Cool name for a cat." Owen shut the front door firmly behind them, having left it open in case Bach wandered back inside.

"He's a sweet old thing, most of the time, hence the name." Jared picked up his bag. "I'm guessing you named Bach."

"Yeah, and you, Dolce?" Owen loved that they both had cats named for music.

"Yeah, although I've had to explain his name a few times. My sister wasn't a fan to start with, but I talked her round, and now she loves it. I lived with her for a while when we were setting up the business, so he's both of ours or rather we're both *his* people. I didn't think taking him from his home when I moved out was fair, so he stayed. I visit a lot, though."

Owen put the kettle on to boil and searched the kitchen drawer for tape. "Is Earl Grey okay?"

"Yeah, thanks." Jared deposited his bag by one of the bar stools tucked into the breakfast bar. "Do you need some help taping your window?"

"I'll be fine." Owen retrieved the tape, scissors, the tea

bags, and a couple of cups from the pantry. "Won't be a moment. I'm having coffee, but help yourself to the tea."

"It's okay. I'll wait." Jared settled on the barstool. "Yell out if Bach makes another break for it."

Owen nodded, already thinking about how to secure the window. When he entered the laundry, Bach looked at him and meowed. He dropped to his knees, picked her up, and cuddled her. "You gave me a fright, you silly thing. I thought I'd lost you." She made a chirpy noise and butted her head against his shoulder. "You can't go wandering out like that. You might get hit by a car!" He reluctantly put her down to fix the window, standing back to examine it when he was done. The job was rough, and the catch definitely needed replacing, but it would do for now. "No more excursions for you, my sweet."

By the time he returned to the kitchen, Jared was by the window looking outside at the back garden. He turned when Owen re-entered the room. "No more great escapes?"

"If she's discovered another way out, I haven't found it yet." Owen re-boiled the kettle. "Is your sister a musician too?" He re-started the conversation where they'd left off.

"No, Brigit runs our business." He grinned when Owen pulled out the bag of scones and put a couple each on a plate. "I see you've heard of it."

The penny dropped.

"No way." Owen had been going to the café since it opened. "Brigit at the Strawberry Scone, is your sister? I love that place. Never seen you there, though."

"I help out sometimes when they're busy. Mainly behind the scenes, though, as the kitchen is Brigit's domain. Being on call as a casual barista for other places in the area works better with juggling band gigs and rehearsals and it meant Brigit could hire someone permanent who didn't constantly need to take time off. I haven't seen you at the Scone either. I definitely would have remembered."

Owen's face heated. Was Jared flirting? "I would have remembered you too." He hesitated. "Though you've changed a bit since the last time we met."

"Beer guy?" Jared laughed. "I'm never going to live that down with the band, am I?"

"Probably not. Sorry."

"I promise I'm not as clumsy as I used to be." Jared dug into a scone.

"I looked for you later that night, but you were gone. I didn't see you at any of Lincoln's parties after that either." Lincoln had thrown some good parties in their early uni days.

"I…" Jared swallowed, and his eyes misted over. "That was the last party I went to for a while." He gripped his cup, his knuckles white.

"I'm sorry." Owen softened his voice. "I didn't mean to bring up bad memories."

"It's okay." Jared shrugged and took a sip of tea. "It's been ten years, and sometimes it feels like yesterday." He looked up at Owen. "My parents died a couple of weeks after that party. Car accident. I kept up my studies, but not much else. Buried myself in them to cope."

"Oh shit. I didn't know." Owen remembered Lincoln talking about a friend who had lost his parents, but he hadn't mentioned any names.

"Ten years ago last month." Jared shrugged again. "So, what are you working on? You wanted to try out some harmonies, yeah?'

"Yeah." Owen knew an obvious change of subject when he heard one. "I'm working on a new song, but it's not cooperating. I'd hoped to have at least the first verse done before you got here. The tune's all good, but the lyrics not so much."

"We can have a go at what you have, and maybe that will help?" Jared suggested. He drained the rest of his tea and picked up his bag.

"Sure. The piano's this way. Do you want a tea refill first? I'm taking my coffee with me." Owen hoped he'd cleaned away the stack of partly drunk coffee cups from the last few days. He unintentionally collected them while composing, his intention to finish his coffee disappearing when he became absorbed. By the time he surfaced again, they were usually cold.

"I'm good, thanks. Maybe later."

Luckily, the cleaning fairy had visited and cleared away all the cups in the spare bedroom, which doubled as his music room, apart from the coffee from that morning. He quickly shifted the offender behind a stack of paper, hoping Jared hadn't noticed.

"Wow, that's a lovely piano." Jared ran his fingers up the keys in a major scale, then descended with a melodic minor.

"Present from my parents. I mainly play violin, but they decided I needed a decent piano too." They'd gifted it to him for his twenty-first, back in the day when they'd thought he was focused on his music career. He was an adequate pianist, but the violin spoke to him in a way a keyboard never had.

"Do you mind if I play her?"

"Of course not. She needs some attention." Owen wanted to see what Jared could coax from the instrument.

"Thanks." Jared sat, thoughtful for a moment, stretched his fingers, and began to play Chopin, a nocturne Owen knew well, but definitely couldn't play like this. He finished the piece and then played the first of Sarte's *Gymnopédies*, a wonderfully melancholy piece. Jared closed his eyes, his fingers moving over the keys.

"Wow," Owen said when Jared finished playing. The music had surrounded him, tugged at his heart, and carried him to another time and place. He closed his hand over his cross, his thoughts drifting to his grandmother. "My gran loves that piece. It's one of her favourites. And mine too."

"It's always spoken to me." Jared sounded wistful. "My dad used to play it when Brigit and I were small. He taught me how to play." He cleared his throat. "This was another of his favourites." He launched into Joplin's *The Entertainer*, switching tone and genre.

"A man of eclectic tastes and talent." Owen approved. "Like his son."

"I try to keep my hand in with the classics, although I don't play a lot of them these days." Jared turned on the stool so they were facing. "Your piano has a lovely tone. I'd love to hear you play sometime."

"No, you wouldn't, at least not like that." Owen shook his head. "I mainly use it to compose. Compared to you, I'm an amateur. Do you play any other instruments?"

"Flute on occasion, but I'm not very good. I started on that, discovered the piano and fell in love. I think Brigit still has my flute. I threatened to sell it, and she hid it so I couldn't."

"She's not someone you'd say no to?" Owen had enjoyed the conversations he'd had with her at the café.

"I've tried and failed." Jared fluttered his eyes in an over-the-top gesture. "Seriously though, she stands her ground on the important stuff, and is good about not sticking her nose in otherwise."

Owen put down his coffee cup, then sighed, picked it up and drained it. "I'm always leaving half cups of coffee around the place," he confessed.

"I do the same with tea." Jared grinned. "It's too easy to get absorbed, right? Especially with music. A good book also does it for me. I'll read just one more chapter, and then find my half-cold cup of tea, and have to make a fresh pot so I can digest what I've just read."

"I love reading too." Owen indicated the overflowing bookcase in the corner. "Fantasy mostly, especially urban or paranormal."

"They're my favourites too." Jared's eyes widened when he saw the pile on the coffee table next to the couch on the wall opposite the piano. He got up, walked over, and picked up the one on top. "I've just started this one. Been waiting for it to come out for ages."

"It's good so far, well worth the wait." Owen grinned. "A dragon in the big city hooks up with a shifter Kiwi, but it still ties back to the original."

"No spoilers! I'm only a few chapters in." Jared suddenly looked shy. "We could discuss it when we're both finished, if you'd like. Perhaps at the Scone? Over lunch one Saturday?"

Was Jared asking him out on a date? "I'd love that." Owen didn't know many others with his taste in books, apart from Jesse at work. Even if the invitation was only as a friend with mutual reading tastes, Owen would take that as a win.

Jared flipped through a few pages, then put the book down. "I'm supposed to be here to look at some harmonies. Could you play me what you have of the new song so far?"

"It's very rough." Owen sat at the piano, played the intro-duction, and began to sing. "Looking in the mirror. Not loving what I see." He added what would be a guitar riff in the bass. "What's that behind me? I turn, and you're gone. A memory, or more?" He hummed the next bar and stopped.

Jared sat next to him. "Is that all you have? I think it has potential. I love the melody."

"Melody's my strength. I hate writing lyrics." Owen screwed up his face. "This bloody thing has been stressing me out. We need some new songs for Frays, and so far, apart from the couple we've already played, this is it."

"What's the story you're telling with the song? I've always considered songs to be stories, but with a touch of poetry." Jared played a few chords in the same key and hummed what Owen had just sung.

"A guy looking in a mirror. He's torn between who he wants to be and the expectations put upon him by everyone else." Owen hesitated. The lyrics hit a bit too close to home, but he'd always written what came from his heart and hoped no one looked at the words too closely.

"I know about that one." Jared chewed at his bottom lip. "And the guy in the mirror? What's his story?"

"How do you know it's a guy?" Owen asked cautiously. He'd never hidden he was bi, although he doubted Jared knew, and he did lean more towards relationships with men.

"Just a feeling." Jared shrugged. "Or maybe I'm projecting." He gestured at the pile of books. "Those books are mostly gay romance, as are most on my shelf. When I write I…." He trailed off.

"When you write what?" Owen's curiosity piqued. Excitement rose. Surely the universe hadn't sent him exactly who he needed?

"I write lyrics sometimes, more poetry than anything, as I struggle with melodies that don't sound like something I already know. I love words and music, and how they fit, but only when they're written by other people."

"I need a lyricist," Owen said slowly. "How do you feel about writing a song together?"

"I'll give it a go, but only on the proviso that you're honest with me if it sucks." Jared's eyes lit up. "What I mean is, I'd love to."

"You don't have to pretend if you don't want to. You don't have to write songs with me to stay in the band. Although that would be great if it works out." Enthusiasm wasn't always enough. Owen had found that out the hard way.

"Okay. I'm not pretending, though." Jared rummaged through his bag and pulled out a notebook and pencil. "I never go anywhere without them," he answered in reply to Owen's raised eyebrow. "So, we have a guy and a mirror, and he's torn between the road he thinks he should travel and the one he wants to take."

"Yeah, a divided road." Owen grabbed Jared's hand before he realised what he'd done. "You're brilliant. That's the title of the song. It's been staring me in the face all along."

"A divided road?" Jared stared at their joined hands. "Pencil. I need to write this down."

"Sorry." Owen let go of Jared's hand. "Divided Road. Lose the 'a'. And I didn't mean to…."

"It's fine. Honestly." Jared opened his notebook, flipped over to the back, wrote the title at the top of the page, and then a couple of bullet points about what they'd already discussed. "Could you sing the lyrics you have again? I want to write them down."

"Looking in the mirror. Not loving what I see. What's that behind me? I turn, and you're gone. A memory, or more?"

"Thanks." Jared scribbled in his book for a moment and then sang the words back to Owen. "Hmm." He wrote a few more words. "I think better when I write things down. Is that okay?"

"Sure." Owen shuffled over so he could read what Jared wrote. "I'm thinking the reflection isn't him, but a guy he once knew before he took the wrong road. They had something, but things didn't work out."

"But he wants a second chance? To go back and fix things?" Jared chewed on the end of his pencil. "What if it's not a conventional second chance? But a proper do-over, with the mirror?"

"Like he steps into the mirror?" Owen frowned. "But then, what's that behind him?"

"His memory and the future is through the mirror ahead?" Jared pondered. "Do you have more of the melody?"

Owen hummed the next few lines, accompanying himself on the piano. He added a mix of chords and arpeggios under the melody line, subtly working through keys on a journey from minor to major.

"Brilliant." Jared repeated what Owen had played with a few mistakes, correcting himself with Owen's prompts. "Do you want to hear what I've got? It's rough, but it might work."

"Of course." Owen waited, hoping Jared was going to sing, but instead, he handed Owen the notebook. Owen read the words, a familiar tingle going through him that meant he'd found the magic he sought.

Looking in the mirror, not loving what I see. Losing you tore my heart in two. My memory of you a fading reflection of the past. One I left behind when I was blinded to what could be.

I glimpse a future, one with you and me. I took the wrong road back then, a turn I couldn't truly see.

The mirror ripples, a hope I can't ignore. Reflections of love from my heart. Fragile glass breaking, crumbling to memories.... Crumbling to memories.

Not loving what I see. Not loving me.

I hold out my hand. You pull me through, back to myself, to us, and what could be.

Divided road. A journey ahead. Alone. No, together. A future shared. Ripples in time healing us both. A love that was always meant to be. A love that was always meant to be.

A mirror heals. Magic in song. Hope together. Love realised. I've chosen my future, made my decision.

My divided road now one.

"Wow." Owen took several deep breaths, then sang, the words fitting his melody, twining around each other, like the road in the story. Emotion swelled from within, and he wiped at his eyes. If only life could reflect song. "I need a mirror and a magical song," he whispered.

"Hmm?" Jared frowned. "Are you okay? The words are a bit rough, but I think it's a start."

"I love it!" Owen looked up at Jared. "Sing it with me. Please."

"I think it's a solo." Jared looked hesitant. "Maybe at the chorus. That kind of works better with two. See what you think?" He waited for Owen to sing again, then joined in at the repeated line, his voice lower than Owen's tenor, the tone rich and warm, the timbre wrapping around Owen like a comfortable blanket. "A love that was always meant to be."

Owen added a harmony above Jared's melody, then rejoined him in unison for the final line. "That was beautiful. Exactly what I was looking for, but I couldn't find the words." He grinned, excitement bubbling through him. "I think we have the potential to make great music together."

"I think so too. Unless it's a one-off. After all, you were already on the road, no pun intended."

"This doesn't feel like a one-off." Owen held out his hand, unsure how Jared would react to a hug. "Partners in song? At least for now?"

Jared shook Owen's hand, his skin warm to the touch, his grip firm. "At least for now." He grinned. "Count me in."

CHAPTER FIVE

The last notes faded away. Jared swallowed, not daring to look up at the rest of the band. The song was good, more than good. It was brilliant, but he'd written lyrics before he'd loved only to have them trashed.

Kaci broke the silence. "Wow. That's amazing. I recognise Owen's touch in the music, but I never knew you wrote lyrics, Jared. The combination… You'd better be writing more together."

"That's the plan." Owen grinned. They'd left playing *Divided Road* until last at Jared's suggestion so they could go drown their sorrows at the local pub if no one liked it, despite Owen's reassurance they would.

Jared hadn't doubted the band would love Owen's melody, but he'd been nervous as hell about his lyrics and barely slept the night before. "You really like it?"

"I wouldn't say I did, if I didn't." Kaci narrowed her eyes. "Did someone trash talk your lyrics in the past? I'm presuming this isn't your first go."

"Umm, maybe?" Jared didn't want to go into detail about some of the guys he'd played with in the past.

"Well, then, they're idiots, and didn't know they were onto a good thing." Clay clapped Jared on the back. "Their loss. Our gain."

"We need some new songs for Frays," Phil added. "Do you have time to write a few more?"

"Perhaps some highlighting different members of the band?" Jared suggested, hoping he wasn't out of line. "This version of *Divided Road* focuses on keyboard and fiddle, but we'll add other instruments before our next rehearsal."

"Or we could add those ourselves?" Tyler suggested. "That's what we've done in the past. Owen comes up with the song, and we fill out the details. I like your idea of some new songs for each of our instruments, though."

"I've suggested it before," Owen reminded him.

"But that was with the covers we've been playing." Kaci twirled the end of her hair, running blonde locks through her fingers. "And the other songs you've written were definitely for fiddle."

"Not that that's an issue," Clay added hastily. "We love those songs, but Frays is a chance to showcase what we can do. And we didn't want to put that all on Owen, but now…."

"I'm a lyricist," Jared clarified. "You don't want to hear my melodies. They suck."

"I tweaked some of what I wrote to work better with your lyrics," Owen said. He fingered his cross. "I've been thinking about writing us each a song, but the thought of doing that alone, especially on a tight deadline, didn't feel doable until now."

"Why don't we write a couple more together and see what happens?" Jared wanted to believe the magic they'd found wasn't a one time thing.

Clay and Kaci exchanged a glance.

"You wrote that one the other afternoon?" Clay waited until Owen nodded before continuing. "What if you write another this weekend, highlighting Phil on guitar, and bring it to Tuesday's rehearsal? Is that doable with both your work schedules?"

"Works for me. Owen?"

"I'm free tomorrow night if you are." Owen seemed thoughtful. "If we're going to learn new songs, we'll need some extra rehearsals to get them up to speed, and for Jared to feel comfortable with the covers we'll be playing at Frays."

"About that…." Rachel hadn't said anything up to now, although she'd smiled and hummed along with the music between sips of tea. "Duncan's very keen for Flightless to play Owen's songs at the festival. He'd be ecstatic if you could play more new songs than covers. We have a decent-sized slot, and this is a great opportunity to get the unique-ness of your sound out there. *Divided Road* highlights that and plays into the band's strengths."

"No pun intended," Kaci murmured.

"No pun intended." Rachel's ears turned pink, and she flashed Kaci a sweet, yet shy, smile.

"And no pressure, of course." Owen took a chug from his water bottle.

"If you can swing it, that's great, but if not, your covers still sound awesome, and we already have a few new songs," Rachel reassured him. "If you and Jared can write a couple more, that's a bonus, but the last thing I want to do is pres-sure you. Get together for a couple of writing sessions and see what happens."

"We'll give it a go." Jared could at least promise that. A thought struck him. "What happens to the songs once I leave the band?"

"That's up to you," Rachel said. "If you're happy for Flightless to keep playing them, we'd love that, but you'd, of course, be compensated for royalties." She looked horrified that he might have doubted that. "We wouldn't take advantage of you or your talent."

"I never thought you would." Jared felt bad for mentioning it, especially considering this might be the only chance of his lyrics seeing the light of day. "Umm, once Lincoln comes back, if it wouldn't be too awkward, if this works out, I could still work with Owen to…." He trailed off.

Bloody hell, what a stupid idea. Once Lincoln returned, Jared's time with Flightless would be over. They wouldn't want him hanging around like some groupie.

"I'd like that too," Owen said softly. "And don't worry about encroaching. You wouldn't be. None of this lot, Lincoln included, can write lyrics to save themselves. We've tried, and believe me, you *don't* want to hear the results."

"Hey, mine weren't *that* bad," Tyler protested.

Phil squeezed his arm. "Trust me, Babe, they were. I love you, and you have serious musical talent, but songwriting isn't one of your strengths."

"I guess I'll leave it to the experts then." Tyler mock sighed and then pecked Phil on the cheek. "Guess I can always count on you to keep me on the straight and narrow."

"Less of the straight, and definitely not narrow." Phil grabbed his guitar. "Tyler and I are off to the pub to get a couple of beers. Anyone else want to join?"

"Sure." Clay turned to Kaci and Rachel.

"Jared and I are off to the Strawberry Scone to celebrate," Owen said.

"We are?" Jared raised an eyebrow. First, he'd heard of it.

"Yeah. I want to meet your sister properly, now I know she's your sister." Owen grinned.

"Brigit's your sister?" Kaci looked intrigued. "Can Rachel and I tag along? I don't feel like heading home yet and I'm not in the mood for the pub."

"Fine with me." Owen shrugged. "Jared?"

"Yeah, okay." For a moment Jared had hoped Owen wanted to spend more time together, although they'd be getting plenty of each other's company if their songwriting took off. Besides, going to the Scone with a group would throw Brigit off the scent of any potential matchmaking.

Jared mentally snorted. *Yeah, nah.*

～

"You're writing songs together?" Brigit pulled up a chair. She was a little shorter than her brother, but they shared the same dark hair and eyes. "That's fantastic. Jared's got a couple of notebooks full of poetry. I've always thought he was seriously talented, but he never believed me."

"Aren't you needed at the counter?" Jared asked. The flush creeping up his neck was hot as hell.

Owen took another sip of his flat white to hide his reaction, thankful for the table they were sitting at. The day was warm, but the breeze outside where the tables were, made for a pleasant environment. "It's lovely to finally meet you properly, Brigit. I love this place. The food is great, and I always feel relaxed when I leave, like I've visited an old friend."

"Wow, thank you!" Brigit beamed. Her smile reminded Owen of Jared's the other night. "That's exactly why we opened the Scone. Although we started small, it's grown over the years."

Jared squeezed her hand. "Mum and Dad would have loved it here too."

"Mum loved to bake, and Dad loved his tea. Not a coffee drinker either, same as Jared." Brigit looked wistful, then brightened again. "I love Flightless. I've been following you since you started. Lincoln's a good friend, and Beth was close to our parents. She was a huge support when they passed."

She paused. "Jared told me about Frays and your trip up north. I can keep an eye on Beth and Lincoln while you're gone if you like. I'm happy to take care of Bach too, if you like, Owen. Dolce's fine with other cats."

"Bach can be a holy terror," Owen admitted. "One of the reasons she's an inside cat now is that she got into a few too many fights. She's way territorial."

"We'll figure something out," Brigit promised. "Beth's still keen to have her company, so I can be your backup plan."

"I'd appreciate that." Owen hadn't wanted to ask Lincoln about Beth's offer to take Bach, and wouldn't put extra pressure on her while she was going through chemo. "Thanks."

"Who came up with the name of the café?" Kaci neatly changed the subject. She'd been watching their conversation with interest but staying out of it, which wasn't like her at all. "I didn't see any strawberry scones in the cabinet."

Jared chuckled. "Mum's scones were legendary; she and Dad loved strawberries, and we wanted to honour their memories."

"I make strawberry scones most days when the fruit's in season, but they go fast," Brigit added. "Would you like me to put a couple aside for you tomorrow?"

"That would be great, thanks." Rachel and Kaci exchanged another smile, and then Rachel cleared her throat. "I need to figure out our trip itinerary before everything books out. The festival is crazy popular, and all the accommodation books up quickly." She glanced at Kaci. "We wondered how you guys would feel about a campervan? You could share the driving, and then that's the accommodation sorted too, especially if we're going to have a few stops up the island."

"It's a possibility," Owen said slowly. "Would we be able to get one big enough for all of us, and our equipment, though?"

"Two vans," Rachel explained. "A campervan for the band and a moving type smaller van for all the equipment."

"That makes sense." Owen frowned. "Clay and I did a South Island tour a couple of years ago with some friends, and we hired a van. There's not much privacy though and we...."

"I'm happy to share the driving in the smaller van with Rachel, and that frees up space in yours." Kaci turned to Rachel. "If that's okay with you, of course. I don't want to encroach on your privacy."

"I'd love that." Rachel pulled out her phone and made some notes. "I can sort out some accommodation for us...."

"Won't Clay want to stay with Kaci, rather than in the van with us?" Jared asked.

Owen and Kaci shook their head at the same time.

"Do you want to tell him, or shall I?" Owen said.

"You know that thing about Clay and I being together?" Kaci looked amused. "We're not. He's got a girlfriend, and I..." She glanced at Rachel. "I'm hoping I'll have one soon."

"Oh." Judging by Jared's surprised look, he'd presumed the rumours were true. "Sorry, I thought...."

"Clay's girlfriend prefers to stay far away from the press, and Clay, Owen, and I have been friends for years, so we never confirmed or denied those rumours." Kaci shrugged. "Might have to change that soon, though."

"So that's what Lincoln meant by I'd work it out." Jared looked sheepish. "I totally didn't, sorry."

"You're usually more onto stuff like that." Brigit chuckled. "Though I'm guessing you've probably been distracted." She stood. "Must get back to work. Nice to meet you all. Properly, that is." She bent and whispered something in Jared's ear. He scowled.

"Quit with the teasing, big sister."

"And ruin my day, little brother?" Her grin grew wider. "Where's the fun in that." Brigit collected their empty plates. "Laters."

"Rachel and I are going to head out too," Kaci said. "We have some stuff to discuss."

"See you at rehearsal." Rachel tucked her phone back in her bag. "And lunch is on me. Call it a celebration of your first song, the first, I hope, of many." She turned to Kaci and then hesitated. "Ready?"

"I have been for months." Kaci slipped her hand into Rachel's, and they left together.

"I did not see that coming," Jared murmured. He refilled his cup from the small crockery pot. "I feel like an idiot. I thought Kaci was straight."

"Clay's the only straight one in the band." Owen hoped Jared got the hint.

"Lincoln said you'd broken up with a girl."

"And a guy before that." Owen shrugged. "I don't have a great track record."

"I'm gay." Jared studied his tea and then met Owen's gaze. "I should be upfront with you, especially as we're going to be working together and living in very close quarters if this campervan thing goes ahead."

"And?" Owen forced himself not to look away. *Here it comes. The let's just be friends, I'm not looking for anything else speech.*

"I like you. A lot." Jared looked away. "We're working together, which I love, but if… this is only for a few months. What happens if… shit, sorry. I'm presuming you might want…."

Owen leaned across the table, brushed his lips against Jared's, and pulled away before Jared could respond, sensing a but in Jared's next words. "I like you a lot, too."

"I need to walk away when Lincoln comes back."

"I thought you wanted to keep writing songs with me."

"Yeah, but what if it doesn't work out? If we… it's going to complicate things."

"Phil and Tyler are together," Owen pointed out. "And Rachel and Kaci are heading that way too."

"Yeah, but you guys *are* Flightless. I'm just filling in."

"I think we could make magic together, like our song." Owen softened his tone. "But if you'd prefer to be friends, and nothing more, I won't push. Promise. And watching someone else play your songs won't be easy."

"No, it won't, but I came into this knowing playing with you guys was temporary. Lincoln's been with you since the beginning. Seeing me up there playing will be harder for him than vice versa for me." Jared gripped his cup. "We haven't spent much time together, but I feel like I've known you for far longer."

"Beer guy. I've thought of you a lot since that night."

"Yeah, me too. Of you, I mean." Jared stood, leaned over the table and caught Owen in a kiss. "I'd like to see where we go, but take it slow. Get to know each other as friends first. We should probably focus on Frays first. We'll be working together, composing and performing. If we cross that line and whatever this is between us doesn't work out, things could get awkward very quickly."

"Works for me." Owen wished Jared wasn't right. "I shouldn't have kissed you. Sorry."

"I kissed you back, so there's no need to apologise." Jared replied with a smile that Owen wanted to see more of. "You're a fabulous kisser, and I wanted more of a taste of what I hope is our future. I'm sure these next few months will fly by."

God, Owen already had it bad. Keeping their growing friendship platonic wasn't going to be easy. He saw a lot of cold showers in his future.

"Owen! There you are!" A familiar voice cut through their conversation.

Owen groaned aloud. Perfect bloody timing. He let go of

Jared's hand and plastered on a smile. "Mum. What are you doing here?"

~

Jared didn't miss the stiffness in Owen's shoulders, and the fake smile he plastered on before he turned to greet his mother.

The woman stalking over to their table had Owen's colouring, but while his eyes radiated warmth, hers didn't. Rather than waiting for Owen to invite her to join them, she pulled out one of the vacant chairs and did it anyway. "I went to the shop to find you, but that nice young man you work with told me you'd taken the day off."

"Jesse," Owen corrected her. "Jared, this is my mum, Lindsey. Mum, this is Jared."

"Nice to meet you, Jared." Lindsey held out her hand.

"And you," Jared replied. Owen had referred to his parents as though they were a collective, rather than individuals.

"Are you one of Owen's orchestral friends?" Lindsey frowned and looked him up and down. "I thought I knew you all, and," she lowered her voice, "it's probably not a good idea to mix business and pleasure, dear. In my day we made friends but kept everything totally professional."

"I don't play in the orchestra," Jared assured her, struggling to keep the annoyance out of his voice. She already struck him as opinionated and too ready to voice her thoughts.

"Jared's a classically trained pianist," Owen added. "He's very talented."

"Wonderful." Lindsey's demeanour changed, and her expression became more welcoming. She dug a card from her handbag and handed it to Jared. "I have a lot of contacts, and I'd be more than happy to talk to someone on your behalf if you're looking for an opportunity to further your career."

"I'm happy with what I'm doing for now, but thank you." Jared pocketed her business card. Owen hadn't mentioned Flightless, so he didn't either.

"You were looking for me?" Owen prompted.

"Yes!" Lindsey beamed. "I had an exciting call this morning. One of the violinists in the Oriolidae Quartet is retiring, and they're looking for talented musicians to audition for the role."

"I'm happy playing in the—"

Lindsey interrupted Owen as though he hadn't spoken. "It's a fabulous opportunity that could be a first step in the career you've always wanted. I've put you forward for an audition."

Owen's nostrils flared. "I'm happy playing in the orchestra," he repeated, "and I don't have time to prepare for an audition. Flightless—"

"Flightless is a hobby, nothing more." Lindsey narrowed her eyes. "This is your future. Your father and I didn't pay for your years of music tuition for you to waste your talent in a… pop group!"

"We're a rock band, and we're going places." Owen held his cross, his thumb stroking the metal. He held up his head and faced his mother. "We've been invited to play at Frays Days in March. It's a fabulous opportunity and a first step in what I want."

"That's great news." Lindsey nodded. "You've all worked hard and deserve some recognition."

Jared frowned, confused by her apparent change of heart.

"It's a shame about poor Lincoln, though." Lindsey sighed. "And Beth, of course. I went around to see her as soon as I heard and took her a casserole and some lasagne for her freezer. She's had a hard life, poor thing, with her husband dying so young." She shook her head. "Does Duncan Fray know you've lost your keyboard player?"

"You know Mr Fray?" Jared asked.

Lindsey looked surprised at the question. "Of course, dear. Owen's father, Howard, and I attended several of his events when we were younger. We even took Owen and his brother, Alfred, a few times. Of course, Duncan's father was organising them then. Duncan took it over after Dustin retired. He's still making it his own." She looked thoughtful. "I should make the effort to catch up with Dustin. It's been far too long."

"Flightless has a keyboard player," Jared said quickly, hoping he was reading something into her words that wasn't there. "I'm standing in for Lincoln until he's able to return."

"I see." Lindsey pursed her lips. "Another talent wasted on rock music." She shrugged. "Well, hopefully, this *opportunity* will get all this foolishness out of your systems."

"Lovely to see you too, Mum," Owen muttered. "I take it you and Dad won't be coming to Frays to see the band perform?"

"Why wouldn't we?" Lindsey seemed puzzled by the question. "We enjoy your concerts, and you play well together. It's just that you have a bright future ahead of you as a serious musician. Drums and guitars are fun instruments, but your friends aren't classically trained." She brightened. "I'll let you know when the auditions are for the quartet. With the Frays festival in March, you'll have plenty of time to get that out of your system, and then focus on your career."

"I can't do…." Owen protested.

"The auditions aren't until July. They're putting out feelers now so that any potentials have time to polish their pieces. Everyone's so busy these days, and their violinist isn't retiring until October." Lindsey stood and gave Owen a peck on the cheek. "Enjoy your lunch. Lovely to meet you, Jared." She leaned in and murmured in Jared's ear. "Talk some sense into him, won't you?"

"Owen's decision is his own, and I won't influence him either way." Jared didn't add, *"and neither should you,"* although he struggled to bite his tongue.

"Of course. I wouldn't presume otherwise. Don't forget our family dinner next week, Owen. I'm looking forward to hearing all your news. 'Bye!" Lindsey turned and walked away.

"Wow." Jared wasn't sure how to comment on the conversation without saying something he'd regret later.

"That's one way of putting it," Owen said. "I'm not sure coffee's going to cut it after that conversation." He sighed. "I'm sorry. Mum sets her sight on something, and nothing gets in her way."

"No need to apologise." Jared put his hand over Owen's. "If you want to grab a beer and talk, I've been told I'm a good listener."

"Thanks, but we've been doing this dance a while." Owen caressed his cross again. "She means well and wants what's best for me, but unfortunately, we don't always agree with what that is."

"Playing with Oriolidae is a huge opportunity, one that doesn't come up often." Jared chose his words carefully. "I wouldn't blame you for being tempted."

"I am tempted," Owen admitted. "Classical music has always been a huge part of my life, but I enjoy playing with the band too."

"Tough decision." Jared didn't envy Owen.

"I might not even get offered the role." Owen shrugged.

"You're thinking of auditioning?"

"I'd be an idiot not to, and the experience would be great, if a little nerve-racking."

"More than playing to an audience of thousands at Frays?" Jared tried to lighten the mood. Shit, Owen *was* seriously considering auditioning. "What happens if they want you? Oriolidae, I mean."

Owen laughed. "Mum's always thought I was much better than I am. I'll audition to placate her and make her and Dad proud, and then perhaps they'll leave me alone to play the music I want to."

"You already have a full plate getting ready for Frays, and working full time at Arpeggios." Jared figured he needed to be the voice of reason, although he couldn't help the sour taste brewing in his gut. Parents were supposed to be proud of their kids, but Lindsey's sentiment sounded like it came with the proviso that Owen's success needed to be on her terms, and his career should be what she deemed suitable.

"One thing at a time. Frays first, and then I'll take a break from Flightless to prepare for this." Owen flashed Jared a smile. "I'll take you up on that beer, and we can discuss ideas for our next song. That work for you?"

"Sure. Sounds great."

CHAPTER SIX

Jared balanced takeaway coffee and tea in one hand and pushed open the door to Arpeggios. He and Owen were supposed to meet that afternoon for another songwriting session, but Owen had texted him to say he had to work that morning until Jesse got back after a last-minute family emergency.

The shop had a welcoming ambience, with bright posters of various instruments hanging on the walls. A notice board by the door was covered in cards offering music tuition and community events. The young man, flipping through one of the bins of sheet music, was soon joined by another who hooked his arm around him while he continued looking. The gesture was natural and clearly between a couple.

Another customer, a woman, glanced over at them and smiled before returning her attention to Owen, who was showing a violin to the teenage girl with her.

An elderly man stood at the counter, and then wandered over to the pianos, and back again. He sighed and glanced at his watch.

"I'm sorry, sir. Owen will be free very soon. You're

welcome to try all our pianos, but I can't give you a demonstration; it's not my instrument." The woman at the counter, a little younger than Owen, looked up when Jared approached.

"I was told the person who usually works Saturdays is a pianist." The man pinched the base of his nose. "I've come here especially."

"Perhaps I could help?" Jared carefully put the takeaway cups on the counter. "I'd be happy to play any of the pianos you're interested in."

"If you don't mind, I'd appreciate it. Jesse's running late, and this gentleman needs to leave to pick up his grandson soon." The woman introduced herself. "I'm Marie. I'm a string player, but as Owen was here and he's much better than I am, he offered to look after our other customer."

"Fair enough." Jared held out his hand and shook hers. "Jared. Nice to meet you." He turned to the customer. "What pianos are you interested in? Lead the way, and we'll go from there."

"Thank you. I didn't mean to be difficult. It's just that I'd set my heart on doing this today, and… oh dear, I'm afraid I've been rude, sorry. I'm Trevor, by the way."

"No problem, Trevor." Marie smiled and gestured to the takeaway cups. "And I figured you must be Jared unless one of those is for me." Her eyes twinkled.

"Sorry, no, but I'll bring you one another day if you'd like." Jared followed Trevor over to an alcove housing several pianos. "What kind of music do you like to play?"

Trevor looked sheepish. "I meant to bring my favourites with me, but I left my music bag at home. I don't suppose you know any older tunes? I'm not a fan of these new-fangled songs."

"I think I can manage that." Jared sat at the nearest piano, and played a scale, then an arpeggio to familiarise himself with the sound. He then played an older song his mother had loved from one of her favourite musicals.

"That's perfect." Trevor sounded delighted, "and exactly the type of music I'll be playing. Can you repeat it on the other pianos?"

"Sure." By the time Jared had finished with the last one, he had an audience. The couple from earlier were listening and smiling, and the girl had a violin case tucked under her arm. "I like the first one the best, but choosing an instrument is a very personal thing, and it *is* the same make as the one I have at home, so I'm more than a little biased." The piano had been his father's, so he didn't want to part with it.

"I like that one too. It came to life when you played it." Owen placed a music book on the piano's stand. "Trevor, wasn't it? Here's the music for what Jared just played. Do you want to try it yourself?"

"I won't be as good as him." Trevor looked hesitant.

"Jared's a professional musician, and it's not a competition," Owen reassured him. "We're going to leave you to it for a bit, and we won't listen. Promise. You want to play it yourself before making a decision. This model's currently on sale, and I can also give you a good deal if it's the one you'd like."

"Thanks." Trevor settled himself at the piano and began to pick out the notes.

"Concert's over, folks." Marie shooed the customers to the other side of the store to give Trevor some privacy.

"Be with you in a few," Owen said to Jared. "Just need to finish up this sale with Veronica and her mum."

"And we've found some music we'd like," one of the men added. "Thanks for your choice of tune by the way. It's one of my favourites."

"If you'll come over to the counter I can help with your purchase," Marie said.

Jared retrieved his tea and sipped it slowly while walking

around the shop. It was still hot, but barely, and while Owen seemed happy to nuke coffee in the microwave, doing the same with tea made him shudder.

By the time he finished his tea, the shop had almost emptied, and Owen was finishing going through the sale and purchase agreement for Trevor's piano.

"Jesse should be back soon, and then Owen will be free for the rest of the day." Marie came to stand with him, looking out the window. "Saturdays tend to ebb and flow customer-wise. Thanks again for helping out. Trevor's delighted with his purchase, and he probably would have gone home disappointed if you hadn't been here."

"Thanks so much for your help." Trevor walked over to Jared on his way out. He'd chosen Jared's favourite. "I have a piano I'm excited to play, and I'll be able to pick up my grandson with a few minutes to spare. All the best, young man."

"You're very welcome. Enjoy. I get a lot of pleasure playing mine." Jared heard the sound of a microwave and guessed Owen was nuking his coffee.

A man a few years older than Jared walked into the shop. He looked dishevelled, like he'd been running. He shot Marie an apologetic look, dumped his backpack behind the counter, brushed his dark hair from his face, and straightened his glasses. "Sorry, I'm so late. I got stuck in traffic on the hill."

"Your nan okay?" Owen asked.

"Yeah, thanks." Jesse dug a water bottle out of his bag and drank deeply. "She went over to the Wairarapa to visit a friend and took on something she shouldn't have. Some friends helped out and we got it sorted together. I'd love to say she's learnt her lesson but..." He shrugged. "She's all settled in at the retirement village again, and promised to only get into trouble on my Saturdays off."

Marie and Owen exchanged a glance and then snorted in unison.

"Yeah, nah." Owen laughed. "Jesse, this is Jared, the guy who's filling in for Lincoln. Jared, Jesse."

They gave each other a nod in greeting. "Nice to meet you, Jared. Owen's mentioned you, more than a bit. I can't wait to hear you play."

"You just missed it," Marie said. "He sold a piano for us."

"Nice one." Jesse had regained his composure. "Sorry again for holding you up."

"No problem," Jared reassured him, "although I'm going to kidnap Owen now for lunch."

"Have fun." Jesse looked from one to the other and then grinned. "I'm looking forward to the great music you're going to make together."

Owen retrieved his bag and took a sip of coffee. "Come to our next concert. We're at Ribbon's Tavern in Upper Hutt next Thursday. Last gig before our road trip to the Bay."

"We'll both be there." Marie made a shooing noise. "Go enjoy the rest of the day. Jesse and I have things in hand here."

"Thanks." Owen glanced towards the door when the old-fashioned bell above it tinkled. "Going now before the next wave of customers. Glad things are okay, Jesse. Family comes first, so no need to apologise. Staff meeting before we open on Tuesday. We need to sort out our staffing schedule before I go on leave."

"Sure," Marie said.

"No problem, Boss," Jesse added.

"They're your only staff?" Jared asked once they were out of the shop.

"Vicky usually works Saturdays too, but she's on leave

today. Judy and Drew work weekdays and are happy to fill in on weekends when needed, but Jesse's nan called at very short notice, so I stepped in." Owen paused to drink more coffee. "You were great with Trevor. Have you ever thought of working in a music shop? You'd be a natural."

"I'm happy with the barista thing, but if you have a casual roster, perhaps." Jared wondered if his offer was a mistake. Working for friends had the potential to go horribly wrong and burn the friendship, too.

"We have another branch in town." Owen shrugged. "I'd love to work with you, but not as your direct boss. Felix manages that shop. I can ask him if you'd like."

"Let's get past Frays first, hmm?" Too much of his life was already tied up with Owen's, and Jared wanted to keep his options for a clean break intact, although he hoped they wouldn't need one.

Hard to believe he'd been part of Flightless for several months already. He and Owen met up most Saturdays to write music, and so far, the band had loved everything they'd composed.

"I don't feel ready, yet I'm itching to get there." Owen drained his coffee and shoved the cup into his bag. "That sounds crazy, right?"

"I feel the same way." Jared reached for Owen's hand before he realised what he'd done and withdrew it quickly. Spending time with Owen was easy, and Jesse was right. They made great music together. Owen's music and Jared's lyrics fit like they were made for each other.

On the days they'd planned to meet up, whether to compose, or play with the band, Jared had a bounce in his step and a lightness in his heart he hadn't felt in years. Brigit had teased him about falling for Owen. Jared denied it but didn't tell her that moment was long past. He'd fallen head over heels that first day he'd found Owen stressing about losing his cat.

Light touches and brushing against Owen had become instinct and something Jared rarely noticed he'd done until after he couldn't take it back.

He didn't want to.

Leaving Flightless already had the potential to break him. He didn't know how Lincoln could bear to see someone else playing in his place, and although Jared had told Owen that he'd like to continue their songwriting relationship, he wasn't sure he'd be able to.

"Something up?" Owen asked when they reached his house. "You're quiet, unusually so. Having regrets?"

"Regrets?" Jared frowned,

Bach sat in Owen's window, waiting for him, for them. Jared waved to the cat, a stupid gesture he'd adopted. After all, it wasn't as though Bach would return it.

"Writing songs together? Playing in the band?" Owen elaborated. He paused on the doorstep. "The last few rehearsals you've felt a little distant. Not while we're playing, but afterwards."

"I don't know how I'm going to give yo… it up," Jared admitted.

"We can still keep doing this." Owen bent to scratch Bach's head when she greeted both of them.

"I'd like to." Jared's heart melted a little more watching Owen's obvious love for Bach, and vice versa. Owen was one of the good guys. He lived and breathed music, and had serious talent, yet didn't let any of it go to his head. If anything, he was modest and didn't seem to realise how good he truly was.

Jared had listened at the front door a couple of times before he'd knocked, content to listen to Owen practise. The piece he'd chosen to audition for Oriolidae was breathtaking and haunting, showcasing Owen's ability as a violinist. He'd be brilliant in that role, and the quartet would be crazy not to offer him the role.

Owen hadn't mentioned he'd already been practising, so Jared hadn't mentioned it. Each time he brought up Owen's parents, Owen changed the subject, although he spoke regularly of his brother, who was apparently the golden child who had chosen the right path in life.

"Yeah, so would I." Owen smiled, his eyes lighting up; the glimpse of shadow sometimes reflected in them gone.

Jared would do anything to rid Owen of his doubt and inner turmoil. That first song they'd written together was definitely about Owen, although he hid his indecision well.

At some point, both sides of the mirror would catch up with him, and he'd have to choose.

Being torn between what he wanted and his parents' expectations only scratched the surface. If Jared's suspicions were right, the two had muddied together over the years, and Owen had lost sight of which was which.

A thought struck him, another complication. "You were great in the shop today with that girl who wanted the violin." Jared hadn't seen Owen in his role at Arpeggios before. "You're a natural dealing with kids. I'm sure you inspired her to reach for the stars."

"I hope so." Owen's cheeks coloured. "That's one of the things I love about working there, and why I don't mind filling in for staff when they need time off. There are a lot of kids who don't get the opportunity to play an instrument, let alone own one. One day, I'd like to do something about that. I've talked to the guys about doing a few kid-focused performances so we can show them what our instruments are capable of and that they don't need to be pigeon-holed. I've had people come up to me after our concerts, surprised to see a violin in a rock band, although it's nothing new."

"A performance to show kids the versatility of instruments that are often perceived as classical is a great idea. Let me know if I can help out." Music tugged at Jared's soul again, now he'd found a group that shared his passion. Flightless were more than friends who enjoyed playing together. They were family. He bit his lip and slowly took off his bag. "If... if your audition is successful, would you still be able to work at the shop?"

And pursue that dream?

Owen grew quiet. He stood and walked into the kitchen, turning on the kettle and watching it boil. Finally, he turned to Jared and whispered, "I don't know. Probably not."

CHAPTER SEVEN

"There's only three double beds," Owen said finally. "At the risk of sounding like a romance novel, this isn't going to work." Naturally, Phil and Tyler would share, but that only left two double beds. Waking up next to Jared with a raging hard-on wouldn't help Owen's determination to keep their relationship in the friend zone.

"I could share with Clay," Jared offered. He sat on one of the seats in the campervan that converted into a bed. "These are comfortable as."

"I tried to find a seven-berth van, but this was the best available." Rachel sighed. "The bigger ones book out quickly, and this did say sleeps seven, although that apparently means three doubles."

"Whoever shares with me won't get any sleep," Clay admitted.

"I can vouch for that," Owen confirmed. "I tried that on our South Island trip and was exhausted by the end of it. Nothing worked."

"He snores?" Jared frowned. "What about earplugs?"

"Nope," Clay mumbled. "Owen's being polite. We had to

explain his shiner to his family when we got back. His mum's scary when she wants to be."

"I can imagine," Jared murmured but thankfully didn't elaborate.

"The van's only big enough for us and the gear," Kaci added, "and it doesn't have any beds or amenities."

"I wasn't thinking about that as an option," Clay reassured her.

"Phil and I could book some motels and leave the van to you guys," Tyler suggested. He ducked his head. "We want to test out accommodation that way anyway, for later in the year."

Kaci raised her eyebrow. "Anything you want to tell us?"

"After Frays," Phil said firmly, "and then… maybe."

"Definitely." Tyler squeezed Phil's hand.

"I had trouble finding somewhere for Kaci and me to stay." Rachel shook her head. "Frays is a huge festival. All of the decent places book out months ahead. There weren't even any airbnbs available."

"Sleeping bag on the floor of the van?" Owen suggested.

Rachel shot him a disapproving look.

"Or not." Owen glanced at Jared. They'd been working long hours together to get all the music written for this gig. If he made too much of a point of why he wouldn't share, Jared would work out why. Hell, and he wouldn't be the only one. "It's only for a few nights, so I guess Jared and I could share. I won't practice my Tarzan movements, like Clay, promise."

"Tarzan?" Jared looked between Clay and Owen. "That sounds very… specific. Should I worry?"

"Mum was a huge Tarzan fan," Clay explained. "That's why she called me Clayton. John Clayton, Lord Greystoke…."

"Tarzan's real name," Kaci added helpfully.

"Ah," Jared said. "Sorry, I should have guessed. I've read a couple of those books."

"Rachel and I need some help loading the van," Kaci said. "Owen and Jared, why don't you take inventory of the camper and check out how much storage we have in case there's overflow." She ushered everyone else out and paused at the doorway. "If you're not comfortable sharing, we'll find a way around it."

"That was almost subtle," Jared said, "and she's right. We need to talk about this before we make a decision. In private, I mean." He looked out the window for a few moments before continuing. "Sharing is the sensible thing to do. It's only for a couple of nights, and I've been told I'm a sound sleeper."

"Who told you that?" Owen narrowed his eyes, suddenly jealous of Jared's ex, although he'd never met the guy, and Jared had only mentioned him once.

"Brigit." Jared sounded distracted. "We went for a few trips with my parents before… This is very spacious and modern compared to our old caravan." His tone grew wistful. "My dad would have loved this."

"Perhaps he's here in spirit?" Owen suggested, wondering if Jared's dad would appreciate the quick prayer Owen needed to survive the trip. He gave Jared's shoulder a quick squeeze. Like a friend would do. "We should take photos of the trip for Brigit."

Jared brightened. "She'd love that. Thanks." He bit his lip. "I'm not going to maul you in your sleep, you know."

"I never thought you would." Owen was glad he wasn't the one addressing the elephant in the room. "I like you, a lot, but I still think we need to keep things professional until after Frays." He fingered his cross. "To be honest, I'm struggling to think of you as only a friend. I want to hold you when you're upset, and kiss you when you find the perfect lyric for one of our songs."

"I want you to be able to do that." Jared glanced outside,

then back to Owen. "I think I'm already in so deep that my heart isn't differentiating whether we're friends or more. I enjoy our friendship, but I think we could make more than just beautiful music together. You're the melody to my words, the counterpoint beginning to intertwine with my soul."

"Wow." Owen couldn't have put his thoughts into such perfect words if he'd tried. "I miss you when you're not with me. I... feel like I belong when we're together."

"Good. When this is over, I'd like to see if we can belong." Jared kissed Owen's forehead. "I'm telling myself that waking next to you will be a good start, even if we don't do anything else. Besides, the thought of doing something so intimate with you, and baring everything to you with three other guys sharing our space, kind of doesn't work so well, you know?"

Owen laughed. "God, no. We'd never hear the end of it, and when we do make love for the first time, I want you all to myself, with no audience."

"Definitely." Jared shook his head. "As I said, I'm a sound sleeper, but I do have a tendency to cuddle. Is that going to be a problem?"

"Another few days and Frays will be done and dusted," Owen reminded him. "I can survive until then; now we know we're both on the same page."

"Yeah. Same. Cuddling and kissing okay until then?"

Owen answered him with a sweet kiss. "As you said, we're already too far into this to fool ourselves that a breakup wouldn't feel like a...."

"Breakup?"

"And there's the reason why you're the lyrist, and not me." Owen struggled to keep a straight face. "You always know the right word."

Jared threw a cushion at him.

~

The sound of Phil's guitar filled the cabin of the campervan and was soon joined by Clay and Tyler singing.

"Wow, I didn't know Tyler could sing." Jared kept his eyes on the road but glanced at Owen, who sat beside him. They'd all taken an hour each at the wheel, with Jared taking over for the final leg of their road trip.

"He has no problem playing in front of an audience, but he freezes up if he tries to sing solo." Owen shuffled closer to Jared. "We tried a few harmonies one time, but as soon as he heard himself, and realised others could too, that was the end of that."

The drive usually took about four hours, but they'd stopped at Dannevirke for lunch to suss out the pub they'd be performing at on the way home in a few days' time. Rachel had discussed booking a few gigs on the way up to Frays and then decided it would be better to play at the festival first and stay a couple of days in Napier before meandering home to Wellington over a few days to unwind via Carterton, so they could call in to see Owen's Gran. The guy who ran the pub at Dannevirke was a friend and a fan, so the combination of a gig and catch-up there was a no-brainer.

"Wow, this scenery is amazing." Jared loved the fields of lavender that soon gave way to row upon row of vines. "I haven't been up this way in years. I'd forgotten how beautiful everything is."

"One of the Great Wine Capitals of the World." Owen shaded his eyes against the sun. "I don't remember much about the last time Mum and Dad took Al and me to Frays, apart from the music. It was one of the last times we had a family holiday. Their careers took off after that, Al started high school, and life… got busy I guess."

"We're here a couple of days, so there's plenty of time to

explore. I'm looking forward to some downtime after the hours we've spent rehearsing."

"Good thing we're playing on the first day and getting our nerves out of the way. I want to hear all the bands, and make some memories." Owen took Jared's free hand and caressed his thumb. "Perhaps, if we have time, we could go into Napier for a meal, and take a look at the all the Art Deco buildings."

"Brigit came here last year for the Art Deco Festival." She'd asked Jared to come, but he'd decided to stay and run the Scone while she was away, so Julie could go with her. "She brought back loads of photos, but I'd love to see the town for real."

Napier had been levelled by a huge earthquake in 1931 and rebuilt in the architectural trend of the time.

"You've been to Frays before?"

"Yeah, our parents took us when we were kids." Jared chuckled. "I think everyone's been to Frays at some point. It's huge. I still can't believe we're playing there."

A signpost alerted them that they were almost there. The tents dotting the fields on the outskirts of the winery were part of a huge camping ground. Another field was set aside for all sorts of vans. The camper they'd hired was solar powered, so they'd booked a site a ten-minute walk away from the stage area.

The hotel-style accommodation at the vineyard had been booked solid for months, although Rachel and Kaci had scored a room at a cute little motel out of the centre of town. They were going directly to Frays to drop off the band's equipment and would meet the rest of the band there.

"Rachel's already arrived, so once we find our spot, we can wander over," Clay called out from the back of the van. "They'll meet us at the winery. Duncan's organised a meet and greet thing for the bands."

"He has?" Jared thought they'd be lucky to see much, or anything of Duncan, over the long weekend. "Wow, I'm impressed."

"He seems like a good guy," Clay said. "He's been checking in on Lincoln too, which he didn't need to do."

Owen arched an eyebrow. "Now, that *is* interesting. Lincoln never mentioned it."

"Rachel told Duncan about our change in lineup and why, and he wanted to help. He has a friend in Wellington who offered to drive Beth to the hospital for treatment when Lincoln needs to go into the office for work," Clay elaborated.

"I read up about Frays and the winery, as I haven't been here before." Tyler added. "Apparently, Duncan lost his mum to cancer, so maybe he wanted to help?"

"Maybe." Owen looked thoughtful but shrugged when Jared raised his eyebrow. He dug out his phone. "The turnoff should be up ahead on our left."

"It's well signposted." Jared would have been surprised at anything less. The festival had been going for decades, so Frays would have the details finely tuned by now.

Owen consulted his phone again, checking the map they'd been sent. "Oh, that's cute. All the different parking spots are named like streets but with musical names. Someone's had fun setting this up. Left at Gershwin, first on the right at Mozart, and we're booked into spot number four at Marley."

Jared drove slowly. The spots were already filling up, with only about half left vacant. The festival didn't start until midday the next day, but it looked like most people had arrived early, which was sensible, considering what traffic in the area would be like soon.

He found their spot, pulled in, and turned off the engine. After he'd undone his seatbelt, he rolled his stiff shoulders.

"Nervous about tomorrow?" Owen asked quietly once they'd exited the van. He reached for his cross, a sure sign Jared wasn't alone in his pre-performance nerves.

"Yeah." Jared's shoulders always played up when he felt anxious. "We'll be fine once we start, though, yeah?"

"Yeah." Owen looked around and swallowed. "I mean, I knew this festival was big, but I wasn't envisioning this many people."

"I don't think any of us were." Clay came up behind them and slung his arm around Owen's shoulder.

Jared narrowed his eyes.

"Way bigger than our usual crowd," Clay continued. He glanced at Jared and frowned.

"Oh, really?" Phil said.

"He means, yes, yes, it is." Tyler pecked Phil on the cheek and grabbed his hand.

"Yeah, sorry." Phil shot Jared an apologetic look. "Fuck, there's already a lot of people here, and this is just the tip of the iceberg."

"We're not on the Titanic, baby," Tyler reassured him. "And I've always got your back." He squeezed Phil's hand. "We're going to go on ahead, okay?"

"They're sweet together," Jared said once they were out of earshot. He let out a long whistle. "Looks like we're all nervous about this."

"I'd be worried if we weren't." Clay let go of Owen and then turned to Jared. "I'm not making a move on your man. We've always been touchy-feely when we're wired. If it's not okay, I'll stop it."

"My man?" Jared bit his lip. Shit, had the momentary flare of jealousy he'd felt been that obvious?

"Please tell me you've both worked that out already, and I haven't just put my foot in it."

Owen chuckled and lightly shoulder-bumped Clay. "We

have, so you haven't." He kissed Jared's cheek. "Still early days, but…."

"And yeah, sorry, I would prefer you didn't." Jared hoped that was okay with both Owen and Clay. The two had been friends for a long time. "Fuck, that just slipped out. You've known each other way longer than I have and—"

"We're all good," Clay said. "I got into the habit of doing it to give Deb the hint that their relationship was over, as she really wasn't getting it." He grinned. "I need to stop doing it. Nat gives me a weird look, too. Hey, I'll introduce you two this weekend. She's coming to the festival, but only one day. Her cousin lives in Hastings, so she's already in the Bay."

"Nat?" Jared hadn't seen much of the band outside rehearsals, apart from Owen, aside from the few evenings they'd gone out for a beer afterwards.

Clay didn't talk about his private life much. "My girl-friend." He glanced at his watch. "Shit, is that the time? We better get a move on. Don't want to keep Rachel waiting." He took off after Tyler and Phil.

Owen slipped his hand into Jared's. "Don't worry. You'll get used to it. And don't apologise for saying what you feel about anything, especially something you're not happy about. Clay would be more upset if you didn't." He kissed Jared again, this time a sweet, brief touch of lips. "And so would I."

CHAPTER EIGHT

Rachel was waiting for Owen and Jared outside the huge old house that held the restaurant and wine tasting venue. "Duncan's arranged a meet and greet, complete with wine, cheese, and snacks. The others have gone in already." She ushered them inside.

"We're a little underdressed." Owen indicated his jeans, t-shirt, and grey hoodie.

The inside of the building was the perfect mix of history and modernity. The floors were beautifully polished and looked to be made of native timber. The combination of paintings and photos adorning the walls depicted the vineyard over the past century. Roses in antique cut glass vases brought colour to the cream walls, their scent subtle yet unmistakable.

He half expected someone to walk by wearing a tux and top hat, complete with a cravat like they'd stepped out of another time.

"It's a very informal affair." Rachel grinned. "You two are well dressed compared to some in there. You'll be fine. Mingle and make friends. It will be painless, I swear."

"You told me that when you pushed me to go see that dentist last year." Owen avoided them like the plague, although the experience was never as bad as he feared. The one Rachel had recommended was pretty good, although he'd never admit that.

Jared raised an eyebrow.

"Broken tooth. Easily fixed once I got him there." Rachel waved to Kaci, who was hanging around an open door a short distance away. "I need to go." She lowered her voice. "Seriously though, don't be intimated by the line-up. Flight-less deserves to be here as much as anyone. You guys are good, and don't forget it."

"She's a force to be reckoned with, isn't she?" Jared chewed on his bottom lip, a sure sign he was nervous.

"Yeah, but that's a good thing, right?" Owen took Jared's hand in his and squeezed it. "The rest of us haven't played at an event this big either. We're all nervous."

"You're way more experienced than I am," Jared whispered. "I've only done a few pub concerts. Some of the bands here are iconic. Lincoln should be here, not me. I feel like a fraud."

"Everyone deserves a chance to shine, don't you think?" A man in his mid-thirties, dressed casually in black jeans and a grey buttoned-down shirt, walked up to them. "You must be Owen and Jared. Duncan's spoken highly of both of you. I'm Elard. My family and Duncan's go back a while. Nice to meet you. Duncan's about ready to do the speech he's been rehearsing for the past couple of days, so we should probably get in there. He does so fuss over it every year and then delivers it perfectly."

"Part of me is scared shitless by all of this," Jared admitted.

"Nerves are part of the human condition, I'm afraid." Elard smiled. "I've always found it bodes well for a good performance. Pride goeth before destruction, and a haughty spirit before a fall, and all that. Focus on your performance and enjoy everyone else's." He lowered his voice. "I'll go first and pave the way, hmm? You can sneak in the back while everyone's distracted."

Owen kissed Jared softly on the cheek once Elard disappeared. "He's got a point."

"Yeah." Jared relaxed against Owen. "I guess so. We better get in there in time to listen to Duncan's speech as he's gone to all that trouble to perfect it."

"And to invite us to his festival." Owen leaned his forehead against Jared's now they were alone.

When they entered the room, a man holding a tray offered them each a glass of wine. "Welcome to Frays. Enjoy your stay here."

Duncan tapped the side of his glass with a fork to get everyone's attention. He surveyed the room, a huge smile lighting his face. "I'm so pleased to welcome you all to Frays Days. This year is special as it's the 90th anniversary of the festival. But, before I continue with a bit of the history of it, I'd like to invite my good friend, Father Elard Reith, to join me up here."

Elard caught Owen's eye as he walked past. "I'm incognito," he murmured, pointing to the lack of white collar, "but I guess I've just been rumbled." He gave everyone a nod when he joined Duncan. "It's great to see you all here today. Like Duncan, my family has a history in Napier, but I'll leave that to him to explain." He grinned. "I do enough public speaking as it is."

Everyone chucked and then quietened to allow Duncan to continue.

"Frays Vineyard was built in the 1920s by my great-grandfather, Devon Fray, and several generations later, we're still proud to be living here in the Bay. We'd built a thriving vineyard and a community by the time the earthquake hit in 1931 and, like many, we struggled to rebuild and keep our spirits up, especially during the depression." Duncan cleared his throat and took a sip of wine. "Devon and the local priest, Elard's great-uncle, realised that their community needed something to look forward to, so Frays Days was born. The first year was small, with only a few acts performing over an afternoon, but it's grown with each passing year, into the festival we have now." He raised his glass. "To the men who started it all: Devon Fray and Elard Reith."

"To Devon and Elard." Everyone in the room joined him in the toast.

"We're delighted to continue their tradition," Duncan said. "I'm no musician, but I do appreciate good music, and every one of you is here because something about your music spoke to me. It doesn't matter whether you've played here before, and are well known, or if this is your first year with us. You're all equally valued, and I appreciate you joining us to make this year's festival another one to be remembered. Thank you!"

Everyone clapped loudly.

"Enjoy your evening, and if you need anything, please let me or one of our staff know, and we'll do what we can to help." Duncan gave another nod and then stepped down, his speech obviously at an end.

"That speech sounded very natural," Jared said. "I wouldn't have known he'd spent days on it."

"That's kind of the point," Elard said from behind them. "Enjoy yourselves, and take the evening off. Tomorrow will be full-on and exhausting. There's a decent bus service that goes into town every half hour." He glanced at his watch. "The next one leaves in about twenty, I believe."

"I see you've met Owen and Jared." Duncan appeared at

Elard's side. "Elard's been looking forward to hearing you play tomorrow."

"Are you a musician, Father?" Owen was curious, especially given Elard's earlier advice.

"Elard, please." Elard grinned. "I don't stand on formality unless I have to. I inherited my great-uncle's cello, and I'm happy to say some of his skill, or so I'm told." He cocked his head to one side. "I need to deal with a few things. Until tomorrow, gentlemen. Have a lovely evening." He disappeared into the crowd.

"Thanks again for inviting us," Jared told Duncan. "This place is great. I love the ambience."

"So do I, and thanks for coming. We're booked solid, but The Sunflower Restaurant usually keeps a few tables free for band members if you're looking for a nice meal out. Tell them I sent you." Duncan's phone rang, and he pulled it out of his pocket. "Sorry, I need to get this. Until tomorrow." His brow creased. "Hello, Duncan speaking. Everything okay?" He walked away out of earshot.

"You feel like dinner out?" Owen wasn't about to look a gift horse in the mouth.

"Should we check to see if the others want to join us?"

"I guess." Owen would prefer an evening with Jared, but he'd also feel bad if he didn't ask.

"Ask us to join you where?" Kaci slid her arm around Owen's waist.

"Dinner. In town." Owen looked around for Rachel but couldn't see her.

Kaci coloured. "I have plans, actually, but thanks for checking."

"Don't do anything I wouldn't." Owen couldn't help teasing.

"Whatever." Kaci stuck out her tongue and then grinned to soften the gesture. "Rachel and I are going to go for a wander around Napier once we've had dinner." She unwrapped her arm from around Owen. "Nat's given us a list of good spots to check out. I can send it to you if you want."

"Thanks, but nah, we'll play it by ear." Owen spoke without thinking, then turned to Jared. "Unless you want the list?"

"I'm happy to do whatever." Jared hadn't touched much of his wine. "Do you want to mingle or head out?"

Rachel was chatting to the lead singer of Whit's Glen, at the other end of the room, her face animated as she moved her arms to demonstrate whatever comment she'd made.

"Could you keep Rachel distracted while we make a break for it?" Owen asked.

"Sure. I'm told I can be very distracting." Kaci chuckled. "Be good, and have fun. Actually, don't be good, and have a good time."

"I'll be the perfect gentleman," Owen told her with a straight face.

"God, no." Jared poked him in the ribs. "I like you as you are."

"Are you telling me I'm not a gentleman?" Owen feigned dismay.

"And there's my chance." Kaci glanced over at Rachel, who was pausing for breath and scanning the room, obviously looking for her band to make sure they were all networking like they were supposed to. "Have fun. And don't bother looking for Tyler and Phil. They sneaked out after the speech. Clay's meeting Nat in town, so you might run into them." She grinned and made a beeline for Rachel, sliding her arm into her girlfriend's.

"Time to make our escape." Owen deposited his glass on a tray on one of the side tables, and Jared did the same.

They linked hands and headed back outside into the sun.

~

The bus trundled along shortly after they found the stop. Jared followed Owen to a seat near the back.

"This was a good idea. We can enjoy ourselves and not have to worry about parking or having a drink with our meal." Jared slid his arm around Owen. Being together like this in public already felt natural like they'd known each other for longer than a few months.

"I haven't been on a bus in years," Owen admitted. "I'm close enough to walk to work, and otherwise I bike unless I'm going a decent distance, then I give the car a good run."

"I work all around the region with being on call, so I've got used to driving, especially when I'm on a late shift."

"Do you think you'll want to give that up one day? Have you thought about working at the Scone instead of travelling around so much?"

"I like having the best of both worlds." Jared shrugged. "But being behind the counter at the Scone is always my favourite. Something about the place feels like home, and although they never lived to see it, I get a sense of my parents when I'm there. Like they're looking down on us, and still there in some way."

"I'm sorry," Owen said after a moment's silence. "I can't imagine what it must have been like to lose them. I love mine, but they drive me nuts. They mean well, I'm sure they do, but I've never managed to live up to their expectations. I'm not sure I ever will."

Jared watched the purple fields go by before replying. "You're still auditioning for Oriolidae. Is that something *you* want to do?"

"It's the right thing to do." Owen sounded puzzled. "It's all set up, and I've been practising. I'm invested now. I want to see if I *am* good enough, rather than wonder if I don't do it."

"I've heard you practise," Jared admitted. "What will you do if they want you?"

"I don't honestly know, but I doubt it will come to that." Owen leaned his head on Jared's shoulder. "Can we not talk about it? I want to enjoy the evening, and then focus on tomorrow. The whole Oriolidae thing is another problem for another day and one that won't be my decision anyway."

Jared disagreed but decided against voicing his opinion. "What do you want to do in Napier? I figure we should check out the restaurant and make sure we have a table first."

"Good idea." Owen pulled out his phone and found a tourist website. "The restaurant is near the Sound Shell, so we could start there first. I'd love to look at all the buildings.'

"What about all the murals?" Jared peered at Owen's phone. "They look cool. And the aquarium, if it's still open. Unless you'd prefer the museum? I don't think we've got time to do both."

"I like the idea of the Faraday Museum. History and tech-nology in one place." Owen sighed. "Okay, not that one. We've just missed it. They closed an hour ago."

"We could always fit it in on Monday before we head back to Wellington?" Jared suggested. "Or we could make another trip up here. Just the two of us." Owen's silence made Jared's heart sink. Had he overstepped? "Or not," he added.

"I'd love to have a weekend away with you up here, a road trip for just the two of us," Owen finally said. "I can't fit it in until after my audition, and… perhaps we could talk about it then? Once we have more time to plan it and look forward to it. By then, you…."

"Yeah, I'd like that," Jared said hurriedly, not wanting Owen to finish his sentence.

By then, you won't be a part of Flightless.

The following silence sat between them like a weight, although by the time they reached town, the feeling had settled into something easily brushed aside. Owen had returned to his position on Jared's shoulder and begun to doze. Sunlight caught his face, softening the frown lines and the tiredness that had been too much a part of him the last few weeks.

Jared woke him with a soft kiss to the cheek. "We're almost there." He'd make sure they returned to the camper in plenty of time to get an early night.

"What? Huh?" Owen blinked at him, confused for a moment. "Oh, right. Sorry, I must have drifted off." He reached down to grab his daypack.

A few minutes later, the bus pulled in, and everyone piled out. Jared and Owen waiting until the bus was almost empty before trailing after them. Owen gave the driver a friendly wave and was rewarded with a smile.

"Restaurant first, yeah?" Owen consulted his phone again and led them towards Marine Parade. When they reached the water fountain, he sat on its edge and took a deep breath. "I'm sure I've been here before. I remember this and the statue."

The statue of Pania of the Reef looked over the fountain and beyond that, the sea, its presence a reminder of legend amongst the backdrop of historical buildings in the other direction.

"We can walk along the beach once we've made our reservations," Jared suggested. "Or we could eat early and then take our time looking around." He raised the side of his hand to his forehead, shading his eyes against the late afternoon sun. "Probably be cold out here later."

"I don't mind a bit of cold if you don't." Owen pointed across the road. "The Sunflower's a couple of doors down across the road. I vote we eat now. I'm hungry."

Now that he knew where to look, the building was unmistakable with its cheery yellow exterior and huge sunflower mural. Wooden double doors led inside. A woman looked up when they entered and greeted them with a smile.

"Welcome to the Sunflower. I'm Adele."

"We're staying out at Frays for the festival," Owen explained. "Duncan Fray said that you kept some tables in reserve."

"You're playing in the festival? That's wonderful." Adele checked the screen in front of her. "We have a couple of tables for two left. One in the corner, and the other upstairs with a great view of the ocean. Which would you prefer?"

"The view," they both answered immediately.

She chuckled. "That's our usual answer, although some people prefer a quiet spot before the craziness of the festival. When are you playing? My partner and I have tickets for tomorrow as he has to work on Sunday."

"Tomorrow," Owen said. "Our band is called Flightless. We're here from Wellington."

"Ooh, I saw you on the programme. You have a fiddle player, right?" Adele looked excited.

"That would be me," Owen said, "and thanks."

Rachel had written the spiel for the programme, which included a short biography of the band and their music.

Adele rang a bell, and a man approached with a clipboard. "Lloyd here will take you to your table and be your server for tonight. If you have any questions, please ask."

"Thanks, Adele." Lloyd was a younger man, in his early twenties, if that. "Follow me, please. I can recommend the steak and the fish. Or, if you're after something else, our team makes a wonderful kumara and pumpkin soup with sourdough bread. It's very filling."

"Thanks," Jared said. "Give us a few minutes, and we'll order."

"Of course. Can I get you anything to drink?"

"Orange juice for me, thanks." Jared wanted a clear head for tomorrow's performance.

"Same for me, and a jug of water too, please."

Lloyd noted his clipboard. The menus were on the table. "Coming right up."

"I like the ambience here," Owen said. "It feels homely and relaxed. I wasn't sure what to expect. I don't feel comfortable at fancy restaurants, although my parents love them."

"I prefer places like this too." Jared glanced around. "The view is great."

Pine trees lined the dividing line of the road, and beyond them, where they'd just come from, waves from the Pacific Ocean crashed against the beach. A sudden memory hit him from long ago, and he wiped at his eyes.

"Okay?" Owen asked softly.

"We walked along that beach when we were kids with our parents. Dad took photos, we paddled in the sea although it was freezing, and then bought fish n chips and watched the sunset." A lump formed in Jared's throat and he paused.

"Good memories are important." Owen reached across the table and took Jared's hands. "Gran says they keep those we love alive."

"I wish." Jared absently caressed Owen's hand. "They are good memories, though. Bloody hell, it's so unfair. They'd love to be here with us, watching us perform, and sharing their memories of Frays."

"I'm sorry." Owen didn't let go when Lloyd approached with their drinks, and put them down in front of them.

"Do you need longer?" Lloyd asked gently, thankfully not asking if Jared was okay.

"We can order now." Jared cleared his throat. "I'll have the steak with some chips and salad."

"Soup for me, please." Owen gave Lloyd a smile. "Thank you."

"I'll be back with your meals. If you need anything else, please let me know." Lloyd nodded to each of them and walked away.

"Good service here, too," Jared said, letting go of Owen's hand. "I… can we walk along the beach when we've looked at everything else and watch the sunset?"

"We can do anything you want to." Owen took a sip of juice.

"And I'd like that, too." He hesitated. "If you want to talk about your parents, I'd love to hear more about them."

"Help keep the memories alive." Jared smiled softly. "Brigit and I talk about them a lot, but I haven't as much with you as you don't often mention yours." Given the impression Owen's mum had made on him that day at the Scone, he wasn't surprised.

"You don't have to follow my lead on that." Owen looked surprised. "Gran's always been far more of a support than my parents, although I'm sure everything they do is because they want what's best."

"That's the way of parents." Jared said after a moment. Owen had said he didn't want to talk about his audition, so he wouldn't bring it up again. "What's your Gran like? She gave you your cross, right?"

Owen's expression softened. "Yeah, she doesn't go to church much, but that's more because she doesn't agree with a lot of church stuff. There are a few bigots in her local parish who made the mistake of telling her what they thought about me coming out." He grinned. "She soon told them what's what. I doubt they'd say anything to her face, but she decided she didn't need to go to church to worship or believe. She gave me the cross shortly afterwards to remind me that I'm never alone."

"She sounds like quite the lady."

"Oh, she is. I can't wait to introduce you on our way home. She'll love you, I'm sure."

"I hope so." Jared paused when Lloyd delivered their food. "Thanks, this looks amazing." His stomach rumbled, a reminder that he hadn't eaten anything at Duncan's meet and greet.

"Yeah, it does. Thanks." Owen waited until Lloyd was out of earshot before continuing. "Mum and Dad and I have our differences, but they were supportive as hell when I came out. My sexuality has never been an issue, although it took them a while to get their heads around my being bisexual. I had to explain a couple of times that I wasn't switching off and on my being gay. I like men *and* women." He shrugged. "They've always been equally welcoming to whomever I brought home too."

"That's good." Jared wondered if Lindsey was the more vocal one in Owen's parents' relationship. He hadn't seen her again since their first meeting, and as far as he knew, Owen hadn't made the effort to visit.

"These days we mainly catch up on holidays, if I can't avoid it. Al's good at running interference, and he's always been there when I need him." Owen broke off a piece of bread and dipped it in his soup. "He and Mia invite me round if I haven't seen the boys for a while either. I can only take Mum's intensity in short bursts."

"I kind of got that impression about her. The intense thing, I mean." Jared cut a piece of steak and ate it. Lloyd's recommendation was spot on. His meal was delicious, and the meat perfectly cooked. "Is your father the same way?"

Owen laughed. "Shit, no. He's a librarian for one of the big regional orchestras and loves it. He played flute for them for twenty years, then opted for something less stressful and time intensive. His happy place now is somewhere quiet, with music playing in the background, with a good book and decent coffee. But before he gave up his career, between that and Mum's lecturing and teaching at uni, we didn't see a lot of either of them when we were growing up. Aunt Daisy used to come around and babysit after school, and Gran helped out, too. Mum and Dad always made tucking us in at night a priority, though, so we never felt like they'd put their careers over us, and if something happened so we needed *them*, they were there."

"Dad was a primary school teacher." Jared had been surprised by the number of his dad's past students who had come to the funeral. All of them spoke highly of him and said he'd made a huge difference in their lives. "Mum was a teacher too before Brigit was born. That's how they met. She shifted her focus to something she could do from home. Our kitchen always smelt amazing, with the preserves and baking she made to sell at craft fairs. She knitted to order too and made quilts."

"Do you have any of them?"

"Yeah, the one she made me is still going strong. Brigit also has the quilt Mum was working on before she…." His voice choked, remembering them going through their parents' belongings and torn between passing them on and wanting to hold onto a part of them.

"I'm sorry." Owen brushed his leg up against Jared's under the table. "We can change the subject if you need to."

"It's fine." Jared wiped at his eyes. "Usually, I'm okay with talking about them. Must be because we're here, with all the memories that come with it." He sighed. "Fuck, I feel like an idiot."

"It's fine, and I'd be more worried if your memories of your parents didn't come with some emotions."

"Including a huge side helping of sadness." Jared forced a smile. "My meal is great. How's yours?"

"Very good." Owen chewed on another piece of bread.

"Do you want to grab a hot drink to take to the beach? The hot chocolate on the menu is calling my name."

"Yeah." Despite the warm days, the evenings were heading into autumn and getting chilly. Jared patted his stomach. "I'm almost full. Not sure I could handle dessert." The portion sizes were very generous.

"I definitely couldn't. Might pop if I did, and that wouldn't be pleasant at all." Owen chuckled. "Can you imagine it? Calling Rachel and telling her we can't make the performance tomorrow."

"I'm torn between wanting to imagine it, and god no." Jared glanced at his watch. If they left now, they'd have time for a decent walk around town and be able to catch the bus back for an early night. "I bet Clay won't be back until late," he said casually.

"Tyler and Phil are night owls." Owen raised his eyebrow. "I could wait to see the rest of the town, but I'd still like to check out the beach if you do."

"Yeah. I want to share the sunset with you."

"And then have an early night?" Owen licked his lips and swallowed.

"Fuck, yeah."

"Exactly."

CHAPTER NINE

Owen put his arm around Jared and pulled him close. "Thanks for inviting me to share in this," he whispered.

The light of the setting sun reflected on the waves, bathing the sea in a mix of gold and red, mirroring the colour of the sky, a reminder of the raw beauty of nature.

"Don't you wish you could capture this in music?" Jared sounded wistful. He snuggled into Owen and quietened before speaking again. "I wrote some lyrics once, but I couldn't find the right music to capture how I felt."

"Do you want to talk about it?" Owen presumed he meant this sunset and the memories that came with it.

"This place brings sadness, but also hope. I'm reminded of my loss and that nothing lasts forever, despite knowing that this landscape will continue long after we've gone, yet I'm excited for what the next day might bring." Jared shook his head. "I'm all over the place, sorry. I've never shared this with anyone before. At least not recently, and I sure as hell haven't told anyone else about how I feel."

"I'll take it as a compliment, then, that you trust me

enough to do that." Owen kissed Jared's cheek. "You're cold. We should get going soon."

"Coughing and sneezing during a performance isn't a good look," Jared agreed.

Owen hummed the melody line that called to him. The sound of the waves and the crinkle of the sand rolled into one, together with a cacophony of emotions that were part of an almost whole. "Damn it," he voiced his frustration. "It's like I can hear the music, but I can't reach it."

"That's what I felt when I wrote the lyrics. Almost there, but not. They didn't feel right." Jared watched the darkening waves and then turned back to Owen. "There's something missing, but not so much so sitting here with you." He chewed on his lip. "Do you think... no, it's silly."

"I'm sure it's not." Owen wished they'd brought a blanket so they could stay longer. The people who had been wandering along the beach when they'd arrived were dispersing, seeking shelter somewhere warmer.

Their hot chocolate was long gone. Instead of coming to the beach first, they'd decided to walk off their meal. He'd captured some of the murals with his phone, and some great photos of Jared, too.

"I have almost lyrics, and you have a hint of a melody." Jared's eyes shone with the idea. "We could write a song together that captures the emotion of this evening."

"I'd love that." Owen caught Jared in a kiss and then deepened it.

Jared crawled onto Owen's lap and cradled his face. "I love being with you. Not just like this, but when we play, our conversation, everything. I know it's only been a few months, but I'm falling for you."

"I think I fell for you that night we first met all those years ago," Owen admitted. "I've never settled in a relationship since. Kaci teases me that I couldn't get you out of my mind, but since we've been getting closer, I wonder if there might be some truth to it."

"She's a wise woman," Jared said solemnly. "To be honest, I've never forgotten you either, although I doubted you'd be interested, and what were the chances of us ever meeting again." He ducked his head. "I might have jacked off to that memory a few times."

"Only a few times?" Owen had definitely jacked off to Jared more than that. "Dreams and reality usually don't mesh so well, but being with you is definitely so much better."

"Oh my god. That's it." Jared reached over for his pack, pulled out a notebook, and scribbled frantically. "The missing piece. Or part of it."

"Lyrics?" Owen had seen Jared write down inspiration before he lost it enough times to recognise his reaction for what it was.

"Yeah. Part of the song I'd love us to write." Jared dropped the pencil and notebook in the sand and looked sheepish. His unsureness caught Owen's heart.

"We *will* write it. Promise." Owen caressed Jared's face, his fingers exploring the roughness of Jared's not-quite beard. "I want more than music with you. I want us to write our own music." He traced Jared's lips, breath hitching when Jared sucked on his fingers.

"You're not talking about the music I think you are, are you?" Jared sounded hoarse, his emotions close to the surface and raw. He took Owen's hand in his and placed it over his heart. "I feel you in here. My heart sings, and I want more. I want to feel you. Touch you." He kissed Owen hard, his tongue exploring Owen's mouth.

Owen reluctantly broke the kiss. "As much as I want to do this here, I really don't want to do this *here*." He swallowed, and then quickly continued, determined to wash the hurt from Jared's face. "Fuck, there's a reason I suck at lyrics. I don't have the words you do, but you said exactly what I'm feeling. Let's go back to the campervan." He forced a laugh. "Can you imagine the headlines if we were picked up for indecent exposure?"

"Fuck no. I mean, I'd rather not." Jared climbed off Owen retrieved his notebook, and shoved it and the pen into his pack. His hard cock strained against his jeans. "If we run, we can make the earlier bus. I don't want to wait any longer than we have to." He searched Owen's face, his eyes heated with desire. "We were going to wait until after the performance. Once we do this, there's no going back. I don't want to go back. But…."

"We'll find a way." Owen couldn't watch Jared walk away from the band, from him, once Lincoln came back. "And whatever happens you and me, what we have, it's not Flightless, it's us."

"We have wings," Jared said. "We'll soar."

Owen groaned. "You know what I mean." He kissed Jared soundly, using the action to accentuate exactly what he meant, and then took his hand. He wanted to soar with Jared so badly.

They ran together, laughing, across the sand, helping each other to find traction. Their love felt infectious, their desire burning bright in the now dark sky.

Lights beckoned in the distance, the headlights of the approaching bus coming to take them on the next step of their journey together.

On a road that suddenly felt straight ahead, its path no longer obscured, at least for now.

Owen took a deep breath, not wanting to think of what potentially lay ahead. Flightless or Oriolidae. Right now, he couldn't choose between them. He didn't want to.

The strength of the sudden revelation rocked him, bringing with it a conviction he hadn't felt before. Whatever his choice of future didn't matter to the degree he thought it might. Not if he had Jared by his side.

~

By the time they reached the campground, only a few strategically placed lamps lit their path. Jared switched on the torch on his phone, and together, he and Owen headed for the campervan.

Owen stole another kiss. Jared returned it, struggling not to groan aloud. Owen stroked Jared's chest under his t-shirt, and Jared answered with a loud moan. Luckily, the kiss swallowed most of it.

Several of the vans on their route were in darkness, their inhabitants either out for the evening or enjoying an early night. Others shone bright, with muffled voices and laughter leaking out from inside.

"Wait until we're inside," Jared hissed, once he could string a sentence together. He shoved his phone in his pocket; now they had enough light to see by.

"Sorry." Owen didn't sound apologetic in the slightest.

"I'll make it up to you, promise." Jared nibbled the tip of Owen's ear, then pulled away and took a deep breath.

"You'd better." Owen dropped his voice to a whisper. "Fuck, that's hot."

"You're hot." Jared linked their hands together, and they half ran, half stumbled, drunk with desire, to the campervan. He fumbled in his pocket for the keys and dropped them in the dirt. "Fuck!"

"Got them!" Owen bent over, giving Jared a good view of his arse. He shoved the key in the lock, opened the door, and pulled Jared inside with him.

Jared reached for the lights, then hesitated. "Don't want to tell everyone we're here."

"I guess not." Owen flipped on one of the small lights by the bed instead. "Better?" He kicked off his boots and gestured for Jared to join him.

"Yeah. I want to see… everything." Jared made short work of getting rid of his jacket and boots. "Want you."

Owen met his gaze and swallowed. "We're not going back if we do this, right?"

"I'm not waiting till after the performance." Jared hoped Owen wasn't having second thoughts.

"Neither, but wanted to be sure." Owen yanked off his t-shirt, his gold cross sitting on his bare chest. Tufts of light brown hair curled around his nipples, with more trailing down into his jeans.

"I'm sure. About this. About us." Jared had no intention of going back to life without Owen. "This isn't a one-night stand. I wouldn't—"

"I know," Owen whispered. He smiled and stretched. "And you're overdressed." He gave Jared's t-shirt a meaningful look. "I want to touch you. Properly. Before was a teaser. I want the full-course meal."

"A symphony, not a prelude." Jared couldn't resist the musical analogy. He pulled off his t-shirt and threw it over Owen's. He shivered, heat spreading through him when Owen slowly looked him up and down and licked his lips.

"Fuck, you're gorgeous."

"Nothing special." Jared shrugged.

"Let me be the judge of that." Owen lifted his legs and shimmied off his jeans, his cock straining against his briefs.

Jared's cock hardened, loving what he saw. He undid his belt and shoved his jeans down, and then his boxers.

"Come here." Owen said.

Jared didn't hesitate. He closed the distance between them, bent and kissed Owen soundly. He then climbed onto the bed and straddled his lap, caressing Owen's face, their cocks rubbing together. "You feel good."

"Hmm," Owen lowered them onto the bed and rolled them so they were facing. He hooked his leg over Jared's. "I have… how far do you want to go?"

Jared glanced down at the floor at the packet of condoms next to Owen's jeans. "When did you—?"

Owen chuckled into the kiss. "You were distracted. I have lube in there too." He reached over and retrieved them.

"Boy scout, hmm?"

"Bloody hell, no. I hoped… I wanted."

"So did I." Jared kissed down Owen's cheek and neck, and across his chest. "Mine are in my backpack. I… would have waited if you'd wanted to, but I hoped you wouldn't."

Owen tilted his head back to allow Jared more access. "Less talk." He threaded his fingers through Jared's chest hair. "I love how long and dark this is."

"I love yours too." Jared wriggled a little and reached down between them, rubbing their cocks. "Fuck." He took several deep breaths. "Talk later, hmm? All this touching. You're going to undo me, and fast."

"I was thinking more of playing you like an instrument." Owen bent his head and sucked on one of Jared's nipples.

"Anytime you want, sweetheart." Jared sucked in a breath. "Shit, you can do that again." His heart sped up at the heat in Owen's eyes.

Owen sucked on the other nipple. He started to move, rutting against Jared. Both of them groaned. "Fuck. Fuck. Fuck."

Jared opened his mouth to ask top or bottom. Owen bit down on his nipple, and Jared nearly lost it. "Later." He grabbed Owen's cock, fucking it with his hand, while rubbing frantically against Owen's thigh.

"Oh God." Owen found Jared's mouth and tongue kissed

him fast and deep, his rhythm matching Jared's. He thrust against Jared's hand, his movements growing erratic, both their bodies slippery with sweat.

Jared broke the kiss, his breath rasping. Owen losing his shit like this was hot as hell. "I lov...." He grunted, heat pooling in his groin, and completely lost it, barely moving away in time before spurting hot sticky cum over the bed. Owen followed a second later and then collapsed against him.

He started to laugh. "Next time, we'll wait for the condom, yeah? We've made a bloody mess."

"That's what flannels are for." They'd have a wet spot to sleep on tonight, but Jared couldn't bring himself to care. "I wasn't sure... I didn't want to without...." He jerked his head towards the pattern of condoms.

"Shh," Owen kissed him gently. "It's okay. I knew, and I love that you were careful. My last relationship was two years ago, by the way."

"It's been a while for me too." Jared forced himself to move. "Clean up, then snuggle if you want to?" They'd talk about condoms and everything that went with that later.

"I'd love to." Owen propped himself up on his elbow, watching Jared wet a washcloth in the tiny bathroom. "I'm a huge believer in snuggling after hot sex."

"I love it even without sex." Jared quickly cleaned them both up and then the bed. The last guy he'd been with wasn't interested. He'd always roll over and go to sleep, leaving Jared alone with his thoughts.

"Same." Owen got up to grab a couple of towels and laid them on the wet patches. He crinkled his nose. "Anyone coming in will know what we've been up to. We should probably open some windows."

Jared rinsed out the flannel and hung them to dry. "In a

few." He climbed into bed and opened his arms. "I don't want to lose the moment."

"You can fly with me like that anytime." Owen leaned into Jared's embrace, rested his head on Jared's shoulder, and smiled, sounding sated and sleepy. "That was music like I've never experienced before." He hooked his legs around Jared's. "And you can call me that anytime."

"Call you? Oh." Jared realised what Owen meant. The endearment had slipped out without thinking. "You are my sweetheart, if you want to be."

"Yeah, I do." Owen reached for Jared's hand. "This is nice. Intimate." He yawned. "We should sleep well tonight. You still nervous about tomorrow?"

"Yeah, but not as much as I was." Sex with Owen had taken the edge off. He felt warm and contented now. Pity they'd have to move at some point. Jared glanced at his watch. They still had some time to themselves.

Low voices interrupted his musings.

"Bloody hell," Owen whispered. "I think I just jinxed us."

"You and me, both." Jared groaned. Unless he was mistaken, their peaceful haven was about to be invaded. "How do you want to play this?"

"We're asleep." Owen lifted his head and grinned, and then put his finger to his lips, closed his eyes, and feigned sleep.

He didn't move from their obvious snuggling position, so Jared didn't either. He leaned back on the pillow, closed his eyes, and waited for the fun to start.

A moment later, the door opened, and Phil and Tyler nearly fell into the van. They were kissing and pulling at each other's clothes.

The light turned on, and Tyler groaned. "Fuck."

Jared made a show of opening his eyes and yawning. "You guys thinking about an early night too?"

CHAPTER TEN

Jared peered around the corner of the stage. He wiped his hands on his jeans. Seeing Whit's Glen performing up close didn't come close to easing his nerves. Those guys were pro and looked it. They'd caught the crowd with their first note and held it with their mix of heavy rock and ballads.

"Once we get on stage and into the music, you'll be fine." Owen came up behind Jared and slipped his arm around Jared's waist.

"You're way more composed than I am."

Everyone had their shit more together than Jared. He'd known how big this audience was, but seeing it brought a new wave of what he was trying to fool himself wasn't terror.

Owen kissed Jared's neck. "Don't compare yourself to anyone else. We're all nervous, and just hiding it better."

Jared sighed. "I guess."

"Don't think about the audience. Play for me. Remember how we wrote these songs together. Or think of us playing music together." Owen chuckled. "Or focus on the good time we had last night."

"Before we were interrupted, you mean." Jared had to

admit he'd enjoyed the expression on Tyler's and Phil's faces a little too much. Maybe they should have offered to give them the van for a bit. *Yeah, nah.* Nowhere to go at that time of night, and they'd all decided getting some sleep was probably the better idea.

Whit's Glen finished their final song, thanked their audience, and left the stage amidst thunderous applause.

"We're on in five." Rachel walked over to them. "Go out there and enjoy yourselves. Once you stop doing that, what's the point, right? The audience will love you, I'm sure of it." She glanced over to where the rest of the band was huddled. "Go join in the band hug. Traditions are important, and besides, it's great for nerves."

Jared had never played with a band with a tradition of a group hug before each performance. But then he'd never felt like he belonged in any of the other bands he'd joined and they'd definitely lacked in the family vibe Flightless had going on.

Kaci crooked her finger at Jared and Owen, shaking her head when Rachel didn't join them. "Hey, you. This is for *all* of us, and we wouldn't be here without you."

Clay pulled Rachel into their hug. Jared and Tyler moved over to let her in. They held the hug for a full minute, and then Clay let out a low whistle. "Go Flightless!"

"Go Flightless!" They all echoed.

Duncan Fray stepped up to the mic while the stagehands worked in the background, readying the stage for the next act.

"Thanks for being such a fabulous audience!" Duncan grinned at the crowd. "And for showing your appreciation for Whit's Glen. I've been a fan of theirs for years, so I'm very excited that they were able to come back to play for us again this year." He waited for the applause to die down again. "Next up, we have a treat for you. Flightless is a band who is going places. They hail from Wellington, and this is their first stint at Frays, although I'm hoping they'll come back next year!"

The audience clapped, but more hesitantly this time. Flightless was one of a few bands that weren't as well known.

No pressure.

"You might not know their music, but after today, you'll be wanting more." Duncan tapped his earpiece, the sign that he'd received word that the stage was ready. "Please welcome to the stage, Owen, Clay, Kaci, Phil, Tyler, and Jared, better known as Flightless!"

"Right, this is it," Clay whispered. "We're well-rehearsed. We know what we're doing. Let's go kick some music arse." He lifted his head, walked out onto the stage, and waved to the audience.

Kaci followed him and took her place behind her drums. Jared was next, and then Phil and Tyler. Jared caught Owen's eye, trying to avoid being freaked out by the crowd as long as possible.

Owen held Jared's gaze and mouthed, "I love you."

Jared smiled, the tension easing in his shoulders. "Love you too," he replied in kind.

Kaci began beating time with her sticks, and then Tyler joined in on bass, playing a few bars before the sound of a solo violin echoed across the stage, amplified by the strategically placed mics. Owen kept playing while he walked out on stage, leading the band into their performance of *Lost*.

When the song finished, the crowd was silent.

Shit. Jared bit his lip, daring to take a look. Owen had told him what had happened when they'd first played the song at Hills, but Jared hadn't quite believed it.

Members of the crowd jostled each other, and someone called out from the front. "Wow! More!"

The next song was more upbeat and highlighted Kaci on

drums. The rhythm of *Off Beat* was designed to be catchy, and soon the audience was clapping along, with a couple joining in the lyrics with Clay and Kaci when they repeated the chorus.

"We're thrilled to be here," Clay told the crowd. "As this is our first time performing at Frays, I'll introduce us, although Duncan did a great job welcoming us to the stage." The crowd applauded. "I'm Clay on vocals. Kaci's on drums, Phil on guitar, and Tyler on bass. Owen's our fiddler, and Jared's on keyboards." He leaned in like he was about to impart a huge secret. "Owen and Jared also wrote the songs we're playing for you tonight, many of which you're the first to hear." He turned to them, then grinned. "The next few songs highlight our different instruments. We hope you enjoy them. And that's enough from me. On with the show."

Tyler stepped up to the mic and strummed the first few chords of *Bass of my Heart*. A few moments later, Phil joined in with the guitar line, the two instruments conversing in melody and rhythm.

"Love you, want you," Clay joined in with vocals. "You're my other half. My anchor, keeping me steadfast and true."

"Bass of my heart," Owen and Jared sang together.

Tyler met Phil's gaze and blew him a kiss during his solo. The crowd cheered and went wild. Writing separate songs for them hadn't worked. Owen had suggested a duet, and everything had fallen into place. Tyler and Phil had been in the band together for years, and when they played off each other, they were perfectly in tune, much like their relationship.

Clay's song was up next, a ballad that highlighted his voice. He sang of streams and mountains and finding love amongst nature. "Your love burns bright. I'm hot for you, baby. A lifetime and future planned. Yeah."

They followed that with *Patterns in the Sand*, warming

their audience for their last song, the one Jared was most nervous about. He'd protested that *Divided Road* was Owen's, who had insisted it was a duet, and as it was the first they'd written together, they'd perform it the same way.

Owen walked over to him and brushed his hand across Jared's arm. He leaned in and whispered. "We've got this. Partners in song, remember?"

Jared swallowed and managed to nod. He turned his full attention to Owen, putting the audience out of his mind. This was their song. Their first.

He played the opening chords and then paused. Owen filled the silence with a haunting melody on the violin, leaning into the mic to sing once Jared repeated the melody on keyboard.

"Looking in the mirror, not liking what I see."

Tyler and Phil added bass and guitar, adding depth to the notes, while Kaci softly added drums. Clay picked up his guitar, something he rarely did, but he'd insisted the first time he'd heard it that this song was Owen's and Jared's to sing.

Jared added his voice to Owen's with the repeated line, "crumbling to memories," which led into a musical bridge they'd added with violin and keyboard wordlessly repeating the lyrics.

Owen lowered his violin. "Not loving what I see. Not loving me."

"I hold out my hand." Jared held out his hand, and Owen took it, laying his violin on the keyboard.

"You pull me back to myself, to us, and what could be," he sang. "Divided road. A journey ahead. Alone."

"No, together," Jared corrected him in song. "A future shared."

"Ripples in time healing us both," they sang in harmony, continuing the rest of the song the same way until the last line of the chorus, which they sang in unison, the guitars taking over the musical accompaniment.

"My divided road, now one." Jared and Owen sang the final line of the song together in unison and A Capella. "My divided road now one."

The crowd was silent for a moment and then began to applause. "Encore," someone yelled. "You guys are going places!"

Jared's face heated. His stomach lurched. Shit, they'd loved it.

"Sorted," whispered Clay.

Rachel had insisted they have an extra up their sleeve, just in case. Thank God. Jared felt raw, like he'd bared his soul to a crowd of strangers.

He could do this. He'd played *Sorted* for an audience enough times that he could afford to lose himself in it and exorcise his nervousness.

"Thought my life was sorted until I met you," Clay sang, Kaci joining him for the next line.

Finally, their part in the festival was over.

Clay gestured for them all to come forward. They linked arms and then bowed before leaving the stage.

～

"Fuck, I need a beer or six, after that," Jared murmured.

"You were awesome," Kaci gave him a hug. "Both of you. Wow."

"You all were." Duncan walked past them on his way onto the stage to introduce the next act. "I meant what I said about coming back next year."

"Well done." Rachel beamed. She kissed Kaci on the cheek and then hugged them all in turn. "You were all wonderful. The crowd was eating out of your hand."

"That was one hell of a buzz," Owen admitted. Every time they played together felt great, but this performance had taken that to a new level.

"Duncan's set up a postperformance space if you need to decompress," Rachel said. "Whatever you want to do, we need to free up this area for the next act. Take a couple of minutes to pack up your instruments first, though. The stage crew will take care of the drums and keyboard."

"I could do with some time away from the crowd," Phil admitted.

"I don't suppose there's coffee on tap in that space?" Tyler pulled Phil close and ruffled his hair. "I've worked up an appetite, too."

All of them had been too psyched up to eat breakfast. Owen's stomach rumbled, and he grimaced. "Lunch, for sure."

"I booked us a table at the local pub just in case." Rachel thought of everything; her concern for her band's welfare was always her number one priority. "Up to you if you want in. Just let me know numbers."

Owen unwound his bow, popped it into its case, and wiped down his violin. He glanced at Jared, continuing once he'd given a nod of confirmation that he wanted in. "A pub lunch sounds great. We're in."

"So are we," Tyler confirmed.

"Is it okay if Nat joins us?" Clay asked.

"I booked a table big enough for *all* of us." Rachel looked indignant that he might have doubted her. "The Cotton Pub is about ten minutes' walk away. Lunch in thirty." She glanced at the stage. "Things are winding up here about the same time. Even organisers need to eat."

"I'm relieved we had the second to last spot before the long lunch break," Jared admitted once everyone else drifted away. "I swear my nerves wouldn't have taken waiting any longer. At least now I want lunch." He hadn't eaten anything since their meal out the night before.

"Do you want to head straight to the pub or find a quiet spot first?" Owen hooked one arm around Jared's waist. "I'll stash my violin in the secure lock up first, but that shouldn't take long. You still up for watching some of the other acts this arvo?"

"Yeah, sounds good, as does a slow wander to the pub." Jared sounded brighter and more like himself. "I swear the acoustics on the stage were a little too good. I could hear all my mistakes."

"You sounded perfect to me."

When they sang together, the warm feeling that spread through Owen always made him smile. Making music with Jared felt right, like their making love the night before. He paused along the path to the lockup, spun Jared around and kissed him. "I love you."

"I love you too." Jared smiled, his eyes softening. "I—"

"Owen! There you are." Owen's mum, Lindsey, called out from a short distance away. She strode towards them, his father in tow.

Shit. Although she'd made noises about coming to see them play, Owen hadn't seen her, so he figured something more important had come up.

His smile slipped, and he plastered on another one. Jared squeezed his hand.

"You guys were great. Congratulations." Howard, Owen's dad, spoke before Lindsey could. He held out his hand to Jared. "You must be Jared. Nice to finally meet you. I'm Howard, Owen's dad."

"Thanks for coming to see us play." Jared shook Howard's hand.

"It's lovely of Duncan to invite you back for next year, although, of course, you…" Lindsey trailed off when Howard shot her a warning look. "Wonderful performance, boys. I was very impressed by your songs. I'm presuming you wrote the lyrics, Jared. Owen's talents lie elsewhere."

"I think Owen's very talented," Jared said in a firm tone that brooked no argument. He caressed Owen's thumb with his finger. "You must be very proud of him."

"We are, very much so." Howard's gaze lingered on their joined hands, and he smiled. "You must come to dinner one Sunday, Jared, so we can get to know you. Right, Lindsey?"

"We'll organise something very soon." Lindsey looked up at someone in the distance. "Oh look, Howard. There's Father Elard. We must catch him before he leaves. You boys are staying for the rest of the festival, aren't you?"

"At this point, yes." Owen was tempted to rethink that idea.

"Oh good." Lindsey kissed his cheek. "I'll text you, and we can meet up again before we leave." She raised her voice. "Elard!"

Howard looked apologetic. "Sorry," he murmured. "She's in her element here, making connections and enjoying the music. I'll come around for coffee sometime, okay?" By the time he caught up with her, she was standing by the side of the building looking puzzled, and looking around.

"My guess is that Elard saw her coming and scarpered." Owen grabbed Jared's hand. "Sound advice. Come on, while we still can."

"Don't forget to stash your violin." Jared pulled him into the building, growing silent while Owen secured his instrument.

"You okay?" Owen frowned, unsure of Jared's reaction to their encounter with his parents. "I'm sorry about Mum. I didn't want to lose the performance buzz just yet."

"It's fine. I like your dad." Jared leaned back against a

nearby wall and folded his arms over his chest. "Your mum did seem proud of you, but there's something…."

"There's *always* something." Owen was used to her praise, which always seemed to go hand in hand with a backwards compliment.

"Your dad cut her off." Jared frowned. "She thinks there won't be a next year at Frays because you'll be with the quartet, right?'

"You don't miss much." Owen kept his tone light. "I haven't decided yet, and besides, as I've already said, an audition doesn't mean I'll get offered the spot." He lowered his voice, in case his mum appeared suddenly out of thin air, ridiculous as that felt. He didn't need her approval. He was an adult and chose his own path in life. "I love playing with you, and with Flightless. I don't get the same high with classical music."

"You enjoy it, though."

"Yeah." Owen shrugged. "To be honest, I hope the decision is taken from me. I don't want to make it."

"You might have to." Jared sighed. "Sorry, let's not let all of that ruin today. Our performance was awesome, and we totally deserve to bask in our laurels for a bit." He pushed off the wall and pulled Owen close. "Whatever happens, and we're not talking about it again this weekend, I love you no matter what, and whatever you decide. There's much more to our relationship than making music together."

"Thanks, and yeah, there is." Owen lost himself in the kiss that followed, enjoying their stolen moment in the midst of all the madness of the weekend.

CHAPTER ELEVEN

The Cotton Pub stood across the road from the vineyard. On the outside, the building looked like a typical small-town establishment, although more on the rural side with a decent-sized field behind it, a couple of Pohutukawa on either side and a huge oak tree in the middle of the carpark.

Jared paused by the front door to read the spiel under the name. The building was old and originally opened at the same time as Frays.

"Lots of history around here." Owen slipped his hand into Jared's. "I like that."

"So do I." Jared had taken a few music history papers as part of his degree. "I bet there are a few stories about this and Frays."

"Getting inspiration for new lyrics?" Owen teased.

"Maybe." Jared wasn't going to admit to anything yet, although it would be kind of cool to write something inspired by their time at the festival, or something about the surrounding area. "I'd like to write something that would fit alongside our beach sunset. Bookends, old and new, or something like that."

Owen replied with a kiss to Jared's cheek. "I see a few writing sessions in our future. I think that's a great idea. We could play them here next year."

"Yeah." Jared wanted to believe there'd be a next year here for Flightless, although if Lincoln didn't return, and Owen left to pursue his classical career, would the band continue?

They wouldn't miss Jared, although Owen's violin contributed to their unique sound.

Jared let go of Owen's hand, and pushed open the pub door. He looked around for Rachel, who waved to them from a table in the corner.

Shit, how late were they?

The rest of the band was already there and had ordered their drinks. Jared hadn't thought he and Owen had taken that long to get there, although they'd intentionally meandered, wanting to stretch out their time together before they met up with everyone.

"Sorry we're late." Owen glanced around the table, froze for a moment, and grinned. "Lincoln! How... what?"

"I wasn't going to come, but Duncan talked me into it." Lincoln indicated the empty chairs on either side of his. "I walked over. He's coming in a moment with Mum and insisted on driving her here from the vineyard so she wouldn't get too tired." He stood and hugged Owen and then gestured Jared to come closer, pulling him into a hug too. "You guys were fantastic. I love the new songs you've written."

"Thanks." Jared hugged him back and then sat down next to Owen. "I didn't see you there." He flushed. "Well, duh, it's a big crowd, so of course I wouldn't have seen you."

"Duncan's got a few VIP seats for friends and family. We had a great view of the stage, but didn't have to sit amongst the crowd, which was good for Mum." Lincoln lowered his voice. "She's putting on a good show, but this trip has taken it out of her. We'll be staying a few days and flying back." He paused. "Dawn and Brigit are looking after Bach between them. I'm sure she's being spoilt rotten."

"Thanks." Owen chuckled. "I think it was mutual love at first sight when Bach and Brigit met. That cat already had Aunt Dawn eating out of her hand."

"How are you *really* doing, Lincoln?" Kaci asked softly.

"We're getting there." Lincoln took a long drink of water. "It's not easy, and…" He stopped abruptly. "You should totally come back to perform next year. That would rate as one of the band's best performances in all the years we… since I can remember."

Jared bit his lip and studied the menu. A cup of tea, or ideally something stronger, sounded wonderful about now, although part of him felt like bolting. Who had he been kidding? The band had made him feel welcome, yet seeing Lincoln again made him feel like an interloper. The dream had been wonderful while it lasted, and writing new songs with Owen would be a way of continuing it in part.

He'd compromise. He had to. Flightless had grown into so much more than filling in for a friend. They were going places, and he wouldn't stand in their way.

"Need to use the bathroom," he murmured, swallowing the lump in his throat.

Owen caught his hand. "You okay?"

"Yeah." Jared forced a smile and fled.

Thankfully the bathroom was clearly signposted and empty. He stood in front of the mirror, splashed his face with water and took a deep breath. Lincoln had helped build Flightless into what it is today.

Jared would do his bit by writing lyrics and continuing to make music with Owen. If he had to choose between that and performing, creating something beautiful with Owen would always win hands down.

Performing in front of a huge crowd made him a nervous wreck. And given today's performance, there'd be way more of that in the band's future.

This was probably for the best, anyway.

The door opened, out of sight of the mirror. He didn't turn, but this time, his smile felt genuine. "It's okay, sweetheart. I'll be out in a moment."

"Sorry to disappoint you, but I'm not Owen." Lincoln chuckled. "At least, I presume that's who you were expecting, and I missed the memo about the specs of our friendship suddenly becoming more."

Jared spun. "Oh fuck. Sorry."

"Don't be." Lincoln shrugged. "And it's about time Owen found the right guy. I had a feeling you'd be good for each other. The songs you're writing together are brilliant. Your feelings for each other shines through all of them."

"I … I'm not looking to replace you." The words tumbled out of Jared before he could stop them. "I said I'd fill in, and that's what I'm doing. I didn't intend to write songs for the band. It just happened."

Lincoln looked shocked, then recovered his composure. "Hey," he said softly. "I *never* thought that for a moment. You helped me and the band out, and that's all I asked. All the rest is a bonus, something I'm really stoked about."

"Let me know when you want to come back, and I'll step aside." Jared mentally kicked himself. Shit, he was making an idiot of himself bringing this up now. It wasn't the time nor the place. "And fuck…" He brushed his wet hair out of his eyes. "Sorry, I didn't mean to have this conversation now. But…."

"It's been weighing on you, yeah?" Lincoln sighed. "We're friends, right? I trust you with Flightless, and Owen. I wouldn't have asked you to audition otherwise. But in doing so, I've put you in an impossible situation."

"I knew what I was getting into." Jared had thought he had, but the reality had been building since he and Owen first wrote *Divided Road*. That song wasn't just about Owen; it fit both of them.

"I didn't want the band to miss this opportunity, and I couldn't leave Mum."

"You don't need to explain yourself to me." Jared would have put his mum first, too, no question, if he'd been in that position. If he still had a mother to look after, he'd be there with bells on.

"Yeah, I do." Lincoln shook his head. "I didn't want to come to see you perform. I thought it would be too hard seeing you up there instead of me." A smile curved his lips. "Duncan was right in pushing me. I saw you up there, and fuck it, Jared, you *are* Flightless. You fit, and when you and Own perform together, it's magical."

"You could...." Jared didn't want to say the words, but he *had* to anyway. Only an arsehole would try to cling to something that wasn't his.

"No." Lincoln shook his head again. "I haven't told anyone else yet, but Mum's not getting better. The treatment's working, but it's only giving her a few more months at most. I'm not leaving her, and... I've been thinking a lot the last few months and talking things through with her and Duncan too. I need to start over. I love playing with Flightless, but I need a new path." His mouth twitched. "You guys aren't the only ones on a divided road."

"I'm sorry." Jared walked over to Lincoln and pulled him into a hug. "I know what it's like to lose your mum." He'd been so busy thinking about himself and his future he hadn't thought about what Lincoln must be going through. "I've been a shit friend. If you need to talk, or just have some quiet company, please ask."

"Thanks." Lincoln leaned into the embrace, his shoulders

shaking in quiet tears. They stood together for a few minutes, before Lincoln pulled away, and wiped at his eyes. "I could have asked, could have reached out, and I didn't." He cracked a smile, his voice still hoarse. "So, you and Owen, hmm?"

"Yeah." Jared smiled softly. "I love him, and I owe you. If you hadn't asked me to audition, I wouldn't have this. Have him."

"You two are meant to be together." Lincoln stuck his hands in his pocket. "I guess we should get out there before your *sweetheart* comes looking for you."

"Arse," Jared said good-naturedly. He had no doubt that Owen knew they were talking and was giving them some space. "So... and I *think* I'm reading this right... you and Duncan, hmm?"

"Yeah." Lincoln ducked his head. "It's very new. We're still feeling our way, and we haven't told anyone yet. Mum knows. She adores him. He's gone out of his way to look after her. Us. He's a good man, and we spend hours talking."

"You deserve someone who makes you happy."

"So does he." Lincoln hesitated. "I'm going to get past this weekend, and then I'll tell the band I'm not coming back."

"I won't say anything," Jared promised. "Your decision, so whenever works. And if you want to blow off some steam and come play with the band sometime, I'll step aside."

"Nah, thanks, though. I think that would be too hard. Though I might come round and jam with you and Owen sometime if that's okay. I won't be writing any music, though. I totally suck at that."

"You can totally come and jam with us." Jared was sure Owen would be all for it too. "We should probably get out there before *your* sweetheart comes looking for you." He couldn't resist throwing Lincoln's words back at him.

Lincoln chuckled. "That's a given."

As if on cue, the door opened, and Duncan poked his head in. "Everything okay?" He sought out Lincoln, his concern obvious.

"Yeah." Lincoln nodded towards Jared. "He knows. Everything. We're okay." He walked over to Duncan, who slipped his arm around Lincoln's waist. The two of them looked good together and relaxed around each other.

They fit like Jared did with Owen.

"You've got each other," Jared said. "You'll get through this. And you have us. You'll always have us."

"Yeah, I know." Lincoln tilted his head up and kissed Duncan's cheek. "You okay with Owen knowing about us?"

"Sure." Duncan smiled. "That's always been up to you, love."

Jared looked them up and down and grinned. "The guys haven't seen you two together yet, have they?"

"No. I was..." Lincoln frowned, and then his eyes widened. "Oh, shit."

"Yep." Jared grinned. "I'd just tell them. They're going to take one look and figure it out."

≈

Owen took another sip of coffee and glanced at the hallway leading to the bathroom. He needed to know that Jared was all right. Of course, seeing Lincoln with the band was going to remind him that being a part of this was meant to be temporary.

Damn it. Owen loved Jared and wanted Jared to be a part of Flightless, but he couldn't dismiss Lincoln either.

He'd stood to go after Jared, but Lincoln had beaten him to it, murmuring something about a long overdue conversation.

Another few minutes, and he'd barge in anyway. Or

ANNE BARWELL

perhaps wait until Lincoln returned, and then seek out Jared if he hadn't returned.

"You were all so wonderful." Beth approached their table, Duncan subtly supporting her. The huge smile she wore didn't hide her tiredness or that she'd lost weight.

Owen hadn't been around to see her and Lincoln as much as he should, with work and rehearsals for Frays and his upcoming audition. He mentally smacked himself. Geez, when had he grown so self-centred?

"It's lovely to see you, Beth." Owen shuffled his chair aside to give her room to get through to the empty spots on either side of the seat Lincoln had vacated.

"And all of you too." Beth glanced around and held up her hand before any of them could speak. "Don't waste your breath with platitudes and telling me I look great. It means a lot to me that I could come hear you today and meet you all for dinner." She sat heavily, waving away Duncan's fussing over her. "Flightless has come a long way since you used to practice in my garage after school."

"That seems like a lifetime ago." Clay sounded wistful, as though caught in memories.

Nat, who sat next to him, subtly shuffled closer. "I'm very happy to finally meet you, Beth. Everyone has spoken about you and how you used to keep them supplied in tea, coffee, and home baking when they rehearsed." She was softly spoken but didn't hesitate to speak her mind. Clay was clearly taken with her, and she with him.

"You were always so appreciative of everything, and it was a pleasure." Beth smiled. "I knew you'd hit it big eventually. Being able to see that for myself makes me very happy, and that Duncan was able to make at least some of your dreams become reality."

"We made a list of goals when we formed the band," Kaci

said. "One of those was to play here, but we didn't think it would ever happen."

"I suspect Frays is merely the first step on your journey." Duncan frowned and said something quietly to Beth, who nodded. "I'm going to check on Lincoln. Be back in a few." He grinned. "Feel free to talk about him once I've gone."

Beth rolled her eyes. "Silly man."

"He and Lincoln seem... close," Kaci said.

"Duncan's been a good friend to both of us." Beth didn't confirm or deny Kaci's suspicions.

"Above and beyond," Phil added, "by the looks of it."

"You can never have too many friends," Tyler said, giving his boyfriend a pointed look.

"Yeah, that," Phil amended.

Owen shot another glance towards the bathrooms. Jared wouldn't appreciate someone he didn't know well interrupting a difficult conversation. "Perhaps I should—"

"Here they come," Rachel said brightly. "And we should order. We might have the rest of the festival to relax and enjoy the music, but Duncan's got to get back to introduce the next act."

"Actually, I have a bit of freedom today." Duncan looked a little guilty. "I might have convinced Elard to introduce the next couple of acts for me. He usually insists on staying out of the spotlight, but when I explained the situation, he was happy to help out."

"That's very nice of him." Beth cocked her head to one side, mouthed something to Lincoln, and then smiled.

Jared retook his seat next to Owen and then squeezed his hand. He looked happier than when he'd left the table and subtly nodded towards Lincoln and then Duncan, who had shifted their chairs so they were seated a little more closely than mere friends would. Duncan gave Lincoln a look, clearly questioning, and Lincon shrugged, then nodded.

The waiter came to take their orders and deliver baskets of sourdough bread to their table, and the next few minutes were spent figuring out what everyone wanted to eat.

Once he'd gone, Lincoln tapped the side of his glass, and everyone shifted their attention towards him.

"I…um… have a couple of announcements to make." He glanced at Duncan, and then Jared, who widened his eyes.

"You don't have to do that now," Jared said. "I thought you wanted to wait."

"It's better to clear the air all round." Lincoln looked guilty. "A part of me wanted to keep some of the illusion for the rest of the festival, but that's not fair to you or the band."

Duncan took Lincoln's hand in his and squeezed it. "If you've got something to say, it's often easier to get it off your chest and just say it," he murmured.

Owen wasn't the only one who noticed the gesture. Kaci looked smug, like she'd expected whatever Lincoln was going to say. Phil grinned. Tyler shoulder bumped him.

"When Duncan found out why I'd stepped down from Flightless, he went the extra mile to make sure that Mum and I were looked after." Lincoln smiled at him affectionately. "We quickly became friends, but the rest is new. We're still seeing where it goes, so our relationship isn't public knowlededge. Yet. But you've always been more like family, so I wanted you to know. I suck at keeping secrets anyway, and as Jared so rightly pointed out, you'd take one look at us and know."

"Obvious as," Phil said.

"Whatever." Lincoln stuck his tongue out at Phil, the action more like his usual self than he'd been in months. "And the other announcement… Jared already knows, and not telling you straight off is a dick move, so…" He took a few deep breaths. "I'm leaving the band. For a number of reasons, some of which I'm still figuring out. You guys were great today, and I'm honoured to have been a part of your journey, but I need to make my own path."

"You're sure?" Rachel said. "We can find a way to keep both you and Jared if that's what's driving your decision."

"Some of it," Lincoln admitted, "but a very small part. I'll keep in touch, though, so you're not getting rid of me that easily."

"We all need our family," Beth said softly. "I'm proud of Lincoln and the decisions he's made. They haven't been easy. And I'm expecting you all to come visit, although…" She chuckled. "You might be the ones making the tea and coffee."

"You'll always be Aunty Beth to us, whatever happens." Owen got up from his seat, walked around the table, and hugged Lincoln. "Don't be a stranger. If you try to, we'll be there dragging you back into the fold. Friends for life."

"Friends for life." Lincoln echoed the phrase they'd used when he, Clay, Kaci, and Owen had performed first together. "Family connected by music, and more."

CHAPTER TWELVE

Jared turned down the campervan stereo and glanced at Owen, who was fast asleep beside him. The last few days had been full-on, but very worth it. Now that the worry about his future with the band was gone, a shadow had lifted from both of them, although Owen still tossed and turned at night.

This was the first time Owen seemed at ease, so Jared wasn't in a hurry to wake him.

The gig at Dannevirke had been a huge success. Word spread that they'd recently played at Frays, and the pub was packed. After several encores and a late night, they'd all stumbled into bed, with morning coming way too early.

Phil and Tyler had left the van in Palmerston North to spend a few days with Phil's parents before heading home, and Clay had jumped ship to visit a friend when they'd reached Masterton.

Jared suspected Clay's absence was in part to give him and Owen some time alone with Owen's gran. Rachel and Kaci planned to join them the next morning after their stopover in Kapiti to see Kaci's family.

Despite the drive being much shorter than their initial

journey to Napier, Jared stifled a yawn. He'd taken over the driving at Eketāhuna after they'd stopped for lunch, although Clay had offered to take the wheel until his stop.

He cricked his shoulders, suspecting he'd sleep well that night. The adrenaline of Frays, followed by the previous night's gig, was quickly wearing off. Frays had been amazing with its diverse range of Kiwi musicians, and Jared was still in awe that Flightless had been a part of the festival.

Duncan had reiterated his invitation for them to perform again the following year, and Rachel had booked them in right on the spot.

Jared smiled and hummed a few bars of the song he and Owen had already begun to write in anticipation, although they wanted to focus on the music that had spoken to them both on the beach that first evening.

The temperature was already cooling by the time he entered the outskirts of Carterton, with many of the trees beginning to lose their leaves, leaving a carpet of rich browns and yellow around them. Jared loved the autumn palette but wasn't looking forward to the usual wet Wellington winter.

"Hmm, what?" Owen lifted his head and started, his words and expression groggy.

"Hey, sleepyhead. We're almost there." Jared consulted his phone to check the route. Owen's Gran had told them to come for dinner and promised a decent cuppa and afternoon tea beforehand. They were a little later than they'd anticipated, with an overturned truck slowing their traffic to one lane not long after Jared had taken over the driving.

Owen ran his hands through his hair. "Shit, I look a mess. Gran is going to take one look and fuss over me."

"That's not a bad thing, right?"

"Don't tell her, but I kind of like it when she does." Owen chuckled and stretched. "Be prepared for twenty million questions, but she'll put you at ease with a cuppa first."

"Lower my defences, you mean?" Jared didn't mind that at all. "I regret not knowing my grandparents that well. I only met Dad's side a few times before they passed, as they lived in Ireland. Mum's parents were a lot older. Her dad died just after Brigit was born, and her mum when we were kids."

He smiled at the memories of his gran at the beach with them and his dad pulling out a huge picnic basket from the boot of her Morris Minor. She'd loved that car and travelled the length of the North Island in the thing.

"I'm sorry." Owen was quiet for a moment. "Grandpa was a huge part of our lives until he passed away a couple of years ago. I try to visit Gran when I can, although trying to find a free day to come over the hill isn't as easy as it used to be."

"I'm sorry I won't get to meet your grandpa."

"When I visit Gran, I often go to his grave." Owen hesitated before continuing. "I can introduce you there if you like, if you don't think that's too crazy."

"I'd be honoured." Jared took Owen's hand in his and kissed his fingers. Whenever Owen spoke of his grandfather, his voice took on a wistful tone. They'd been close, and he missed him.

"Left here." Owen pointed to the street sign Jared had been keeping an eye out for. "And then first on the right. She's about halfway down. There's a good-sized concrete pad to the left of the driveway in front of the house, so we can park there."

His gran's house was a modest old-style villa with a huge tree out the front and a gravel garden with a few shrubs running along the right side of the drive. Jared eased the campervan up the driveway, following Owen's parking directions.

As soon as he stopped the engine, an older lady Jared recognised from the photos Owen had shown him, opened the front door and stood there smiling.

"Gran, we're here!" Owen climbed down from the van and met his gran mid-way. "I've missed you." They pulled each other into a hug and held on tightly.

"Missed you too." Owen's gran held him out at arm's length and looked him up and down. "You're tired, and you've lost weight. We'll have to do something about that." She grinned when she saw Jared. "You must be Jared. I've been very much looking forward to meeting you. I'm Irene, but you can call me Gran if you like. The rest of the band does. After all, you're family in all the ways that count."

"It's nice to meet you too, Ir… Gran." Jared hung back, not wanting to interfere in their reunion, but Gran gestured for him to come closer.

She then gave him the same up-and-down exam she'd done Owen. "You're keeping him, right?"

"Yes." Owen held out his hand for Jared. "I am. You'll see a lot more of us. I promise."

"You boys need to live your lives too. That's important." Gran smiled again, her eyes crinkling.

Jared decided he liked her already. "Owen often speaks of you. I can see why."

"If he gives you up, I'll have you." Gran laughed at Owen's reaction. "Silly boy. I'm just teasing as well, you know. No one will ever replace my Richard." She waited for them to grab their packs from the van. "Being happy and content with your life and those in it, is what truly matters. Everything else is mere detail."

"My parents would have agreed." Jared followed Owen's lead and put his pack by the door. He sniffed the air. "Wow, what is that smell? It reminds me of the café."

"Those are Gran's famous lemon scones." Owen grinned. "Do you want help with the tea, Gran?"

"I'm fine. Sit and get comfortable while I bring things

through. I won't be long." Gran disappeared into the kitchen. "Shoo the cat off the sofa if he won't move."

A black cat looked up when they entered the living room but didn't shift from his position on the arm of the sofa. Owen sat next to him, patted him, and was rewarded with a loud purr.

"This is Kijé." Owen laughed at Jared's reaction. "He's named after the imaginary guy in Prokofiev's suite."

"I know the one. I never thought of naming a cat after him, though. Brilliant." Jared took the empty spot next to Owen and looked around the room.

A piano stood in the corner, with an instrument case next to that.

"That's my viola, although I don't play it very often these days." Gran set a tray of scones and tea in front of them. "I taught piano for many years too. This house used to be busy with children coming for their lessons. I only gave up a few years ago." A shadow crossed her face. "My Richard played too. I haven't had the heart to open the piano since he passed."

"I could play if you'd like," Jared offered and then wondered if he'd stepped out of line.

"That would be wonderful, thank you!" Gran looked delighted. "Lindsey tells me you play keyboard for the band." She sighed. "Poor Lincoln and Beth. I should take a day trip over the hill and visit one day. Perhaps I'll hitch a ride with Jesse's young man. He works in the library in Featherston, you know."

"I'd be happy to give you a lift if I'm over here," Jared offered. "I sometimes fill in for a morning or afternoon shift in some of the local cafés."

"Jared and his sister own The Strawberry Scone," Owen added. "I never made the connection until he told me."

"Meetings happen when they're meant to." Gran poured

the tea. "I've been in the Scone several times. Your sister's Brigit, then?"

Jared nodded. He didn't remember seeing her in there either. Perhaps it was time he spent more time at the Scone and less filling in everywhere else.

"Lovely girl." Gran munched her scone, smiling when Jared looked around the room at all the photos on the wall. One of Gran and an older man took centre stage on the top of the piano, obviously playing a duet together. "That's my Richard."

"I can see the resemblance between him and Owen." Jared put down his cup and wandered over to the wall.

A much younger Lindsey smiled down at him, although he recognised the fierce determination in her eyes still from the couple of times they'd met.

"My Lindsey has always had a mind of her own," Gran said. "She means well and has a kind heart, but once she sets her sights on a goal, she doesn't waver, even if it's one she shouldn't be pursuing."

"To be honest, I thought you were Howard's mum," Jared admitted, although now he'd seen a photo of Richard, he could see the resemblance.

Gran chuckled. "We're a laid-back lot, free-spirited, you might say, so he fits in well. Lindsey's more like her dad, who knew what he wanted and went for it. He was a hard worker and much loved, once you got through the barriers he erected. Not many had the privilege to see his soft side, but it was there all right."

"I'll take your word on that." Jared figured he'd need to dig deep to see that in Lindsey. "Owen's more like you, although…."

"Oh, I definitely take after Gran's side of the family." Owen ran his hand over his cross.

Gran's expression soured. "We used to be proud churchgoers back in the day, but not after some of the bigots in the congregation made their views known." She snorted. "Someone I thought a friend said that she'd prefer her daughter to become pregnant out of wedlock than announce she was gay. I told her I'd support my family in either of those situations."

"I still remember what she said when she gave me this." Owen let go of his cross.

"You don't need a church to have faith," Gran said. "It comes from within, not from the words of people who should know better."

"Love is love." Jared didn't remember Owen ever talking about attending church, but then he didn't either.

"Exactly." Gran gave them both a look. "Eat up. I have a lovely vegetable soup for later, and some bread from the bakery to go with it, so we'll need a gap between this and then to fit it all in."

～

When Owen woke the next morning, Jared still slumbered beside him. Careful not to disturb him, Owen threw on a sweatshirt over his sleep pants and wandered out to the kitchen, looking for coffee.

"Coffee's almost brewed." Gran looked up from her steaming cup of tea. "I figured your young man might sleep later. He looked exhausted last night."

"Yeah, he did the final bit of the driving, so he didn't have a chance to nap like I did." Owen yawned and popped a couple of slices of bread into the toaster.

"I like him." Gran gestured towards the fridge. "I tried my hand at some feijoa jam. It's good. If you want to give it a try."

"Sure, thanks." Owen always enjoyed Gran's jams and

preserves. He fished out the margarine and jam and appreciatively sniffed the wonderful coffee aroma filling the kitchen. "We both had fun last night. It's been a while since I've played some of those older songs."

Gran smiled. "I've missed playing my viola. Our session was just what I needed to pull it out again. Jared's got some talent too."

They'd begun their impromptu jam session with some classical music, and then moved through several decades, covering their favourites. Jared had played for Gran first, at her insistence. Owen had joined in with his violin, with them both finally convincing Gran to pull out her viola.

"He's seriously talented." Owen took a sip of coffee and sighed in contentment. She'd always made it just right. "We're lucky to have him in the band. When Lincoln said he'd have to take a break, I was worried that we wouldn't find anyone good enough to replace him."

"Have you thought about how they'd replace you if you left?" Gran never beat around the bush.

"Who said I was thinking about leaving?" Owen asked cautiously, although the answer was a no-brainer.

"Lindsey seems to think your audition for Oriolidae is a formality and that you're a shoo-in for the position."

"I hope she's not spreading that around." Owen frowned. "I'm not the only one auditioning. There are other, way better, violinists out there."

"You're a brilliant violinist." Gran didn't throw around compliments without good reason. "This is one of the few times, of late, that I agree with your mum."

Owen collected his thoughts while he added spread to his toast. "It's a…chance to try. I doubt I'll get it."

"Do you want to?"

"Audition or play for them?"

"Both." Gran fixed him with one of her trademark intense

gazes. "Correct me if I'm wrong, but I thought you were happy with your life. You love working in the shop, and Flightless has always been your dream."

"Yeah, I am. It is." Owen put down his cup and bit his lip. "I honestly don't know what to do, Gran. Mum and Dad have always wanted me to make them proud and have a successful music career like Al. I don't want to disappoint them."

"Owen." Gran shook her head. "They *are* proud of you, and even if that wasn't the case, it's never a good idea to live your life to please others. At the end of the day, you're the one living with your decisions, and it's important to follow your passion, and be true to yourself."

"How am I supposed to know what that is?" Owen finally voiced what he'd been too scared to say aloud. "I love Flightless, and I never thought we'd play at Frays, but what if that's our only shot at making it? I don't want to work at Arpeggios forever, but I need to make a living. What if I turn down this opportunity, and then everything else crashes and burns?"

"Does that include me?" Jared asked from the doorway.

Owen whirled around, his words echoing through his mind. "No! Of course not. I didn't mean... I was talking about the band. Not us."

"Follow your heart and your passion. They don't necessarily need to be the same, but being on the same page is important." Gran quietly got up, kissed Owen on the head, and deposited her empty cup in the sink. "I'm going to shower. I think you boys need to talk without an audience." She glanced at Jared. "There's still plenty of tea in the pot. Conversation goes better with tea, I've found."

"Thanks." Jared didn't speak again until she'd left. "I can understand why you'd be torn between the band and the quartet."

Owen poured him some tea. "Do you want some toast?"

"Later." Jared walked over to Owen and slipped his arm

around Owen's waist. "Being with you doesn't depend on Flightless." He leaned his head on Owen's shoulder. "You know that, right? I want a future with you, whatever that looks like."

"I don't know what I want." Owen turned in Jared's embrace and kissed him softly on the lips. "Can we sit on the sofa for a while? I think I need to get my thoughts out." He should have done it weeks ago.

"I'm happy to listen if that's what you need." Jared reached around Owen and grabbed both their cups. "Do you want the rest of your toast?"

"I'm not sure I could stomach all of it. Split?"

"Of course." Jared led them over to the sofa. "I've been worried about you." He took a slow sip of tea, and then leaned back on the sofa, inviting Owen to move closer. "Sometimes, I think I'd do anything to have my parents back and make them proud, but they'd want me to live my life, not theirs."

"I wish I'd been able to meet them." Owen settled into Jared's arms, leaning back against his chest. "This isn't only about making my parents proud of me." He didn't share Gran's conviction that they already were. "I honestly don't know what I'll do if I ace this audition. Classical music fills a hole in my soul, but Flightless fills some of it too, as do you." He added hurriedly. "I'm not about to give you up, but I thought I was doing okay with the rest of it, walking a fine line between the two and not having to choose."

"You said you wanted more out of life than working in a music shop?" Jared prompted when Owen lapsed into silence.

"Yeah. I enjoy helping people with their musical journey, but I don't own the shop, only manage it, and…" Owen hadn't mentioned this to anyone yet. "The pile of paperwork that goes with that keeps growing, so I'm spending less time doing the part of the job I love. I'm not cut out for accounts and staff management. It's not what I signed up for." He'd taken the promotion because the money was better, and he had a mortgage.

"If you could imagine your life in a year's time and everything you want from that, what would it look like?"

Owen closed his eyes, fighting the urge to shrug and sidestep the question. "We'd still be together."

"And?" Jared prompted.

"I wouldn't be working in the shop." Owen sighed. "The rest of it… I honestly don't know. I guess my road is rather more divided than I thought it was."

"I'll support whatever decision you make, but you have to be the one to make it, sweetheart." Jared ran his fingers through Owen's hair. "I'm sure the band would support you either way too."

"Did I mention I suck at this?" Owen opened his eyes and sipped his coffee.

"I kind of got that impression without you saying anything."

"Thanks." Owen didn't take the comment as an insult, but as a statement of fact. "I'm kind of hoping the quartet doesn't want me, and that makes the decision for me."

"It won't solve your issues with the shop." Jared sounded thoughtful. "What if you told management that you wanted your original position back? Or don't you want to work there at all?"

"If I gave up my position, I'd leave." Owen didn't want that awkward conversation. "I've loved being there, but it's time to move on, yet I need something to move on to."

"That makes sense." Jared's fingers stilled.

"Whatever it is, spit it out." Owen could read the sudden silence for the hesitation it was.

"I think… and in saying this, I realise I haven't been with

Flightless that long… but these guys love you. Maybe talk to them? Tell them how you feel? That way, if you decide to leave, it's not going to be out of left field."

"Okay." Owen wriggled back against Jared and stole a corner of toast. "I hate that you're right, but you are." He chewed thoughtfully. "But let me get through this audition first, okay? I can't go into that half-cocked. They'll pick up on it immediately, and if I don't give it my all, what's the point of trying?"

"I won't be telling the band anything." Jared sat up straighter. "This is your decision. We've talked, but that doesn't give me the right to tell anyone else about it."

"Thanks." Owen took Jared's cup and put it down. He swallowed his mouthful of toast. "There are a lot of reasons why I love you. This is one of them."

"Only one?" Jared swallowed, his Adam's apple moving up and down. "How long do you think Gran's going to take in the shower?" He ran his hand over Owen's thigh. "I can be quiet if you can."

"She's giving us space." Owen turned to straddle Jared. "For as long as we need."

"Good." Jared glanced at the living room door. "Perhaps we should move into the bedroom, hmm? Your gran, walking in on us having sex, isn't high on my to-do list for today. Although doing you, definitely is." He slowly licked his lips, the actions going immediately to Owen's groin.

"Totally. To both of those." Owen reluctantly got up to move.

Someone thumped on the front door before he got that far.

"Shit," he groaned.

"Whoever that is, they owe us." Jared glanced at the clock on the wall. "I guess it is ten already. It's not *that* early."

"They only needed to wait another ten minutes." Owen shoved down his annoyance and opened the door.

Rachel stood there with a grin, Kaci bubbling with excitement behind her. "I have news!" She peered past Owen. "You all decent in there?"

"We are now." Jared joined Owen at the door. "What's up?"

"This is big. Hi, Gran. Good to see you again." Rachel hugged Gran when she came down the hallway to meet them at the door.

"Come in, both of you. I'll put on more tea and coffee." Gran disappeared into the kitchen.

Rachel retrieved her tablet from her bag. "I'm going to set up a video call to everyone."

"This is *really* big," Kaci confirmed. Her eyes shone, her face animated. "And fuck, so exciting. I still can't believe it."

"Not helping, hon," Rachel murmured.

The video call connected immediately. Obviously, everyone else had been forewarned.

"We were almost here, so no point phoning you first," Kaci explained.

"What's up?" Clay echoed Jared's earlier question.

"Brace yourselves." Rachel's normally calm demeanour gave way to excitement. "Your performance at Frays was great, and way successful. I was contacted this morning with an offer I couldn't turn down."

"But—" Owen started to protest that it wasn't like her to accept something without checking in first.

"Of course, I told them I'd ask you first." Rachel shot him a glare that suggested she knew exactly where his thoughts had gone.

"Don't leave us in suspense too long," Tyler said.

"We… as in Flightless, have been invited to play at Rocktoberfest!"

CHAPTER THIRTEEN

"Rocktoberfest? Shit. Really?" Jared reached for Owen's hand and squeezed it, needing the touch to reassure himself he wasn't dreaming.

Frays had been the chance of a lifetime, but that performance paled against playing for Rocktoberfest in the States. Jared hadn't left New Zealand before, although he had a passport. This was huge, bigger than the Nevada Desert, where the annual event was held.

"No, I'm just kidding." Rachel rolled her eyes. "Of course, really. One of their talent scouts saw you perform and was very impressed. They loved your sound and songs." She let off a long breath.

Gran pushed a cup of coffee towards her. "You look like you need this."

"Thanks." Rachel took a few sips before continuing. "So, I need a vote. We all need to be in, or this isn't a go. All or nothing, right?"

"Right." Clay raised his hand. "I'm in."

Tyler and Phil raised theirs. "So are we," Phil said. "Wow, Rocktoberfest. Going there has been on my bucket list since it started. I never dreamed I'd get to play there." He pulled Tyler close and kissed him hard.

Kaci chuckled. "I'm definitely in. We'd be crazy to turn it down, right?"

"Right." Jared raised his hand, shoving down the moment of guilt that he'd be the one going, not Lincoln. But, he *was* Flightless now.

Everyone turned to look at Owen, his silence loud in the excitement.

Jared squeezed Owen's hand again. "Rip off the bandage, sweetheart. It will go easier." He wasn't pushing Owen into this. Given the situation, he had no choice but to tell them about his upcoming audition now instead of later.

"First off…" Owen cleared his throat. "I'm definitely in. We'd be crazy to turn this down. I'll make it work. Somehow."

"Make what work?" Kaci frowned. "Is this something to do with what's been bothering you the last month or so?"

"I can never hide anything from you." Owen's tone was light, but the strain in his voice came through.

"We've been friends way too long," Kaci agreed. "Now, spill. It can't be that bad, right?"

"I have an audition with Oriolidae in July. One of their violinists is leaving." Owen leaned back against Jared. "Fucking awful timing, I know, and I'm sorry. She's not retiring until October, so I'm sure we can do this first, whatever way it goes."

"And then what?" Rachel sounded concerned. "You're a talented violinist. You need to be able to follow your dreams."

"Yeah, well, I'm not sure what those dreams are." Owen gripped his cross. "I love you guys and playing for Flightless. It's too much a part of my life to give it up. But… I need to do this audition to see if I'm good enough and to…."

Gran narrowed her eyes but said nothing. Jared bit his lip,

following her lead. Owen's issues with his mum were private, although he doubted anyone who knew her had a fair idea what, or rather who had driven Owen's need to audition.

"You'll ace the audition." Clay nodded sagely. "And if you decide you want a change, at least Flightless has gone out with one hell of a bang. Works for me."

"You're sure?" Owen asked. "I don't want to break up the band. You could still continue without—"

"Let's focus on this first, hmm?" Rachel suggested. "So, whatever happens, we're still going to Rocktoberfest. Whether it's our swan song or the start of something bigger, we can throw it in the too-hard basket for later." She fixed each one of them in turn with her serious look, one that everyone was clued up enough not to ignore. "However, if we do this, we need to go all in and perform our very best. No half-arsed performance or rehearsals." She turned to Owen. "Will that be an issue? Can you manage to juggle both?"

"Yes. Definitely. I'll tell the orchestra I'm taking a few months off. That will free up some time. I've already missed the first couple of rehearsals for the next concert anyway." Owen straightened his shoulders and let go of his cross. "I'm fully on board. Promise."

"Right then." Rachel's serious look morphed into a grin. "I'll tell them Flightless will be performing at this year's Rocktoberfest."

"One more thing." Tyler looked embarrassed but ploughed on when he had everyone's attention. "How are we going to afford to get there? It's expensive to get over there, let alone everything else that goes with that."

Gran chuckled. "That's an easy one, lad. We do what every group has done for generations when they're aiming for an expensive goal. We fundraise."

"I don't think a few cake stalls are going to cut it." Owen

shook his head. "I have some savings, so I might be able to scrape together an airfare, but…."

"That's a brilliant idea." Rachel sounded delighted. "We could do some benefit concerts. And raffle tickets. Everyone loves those. And perhaps even a few cake stalls. Get your thinking hats on. Hell, I'll take out a loan if I have to."

"No loans." Clay shook his head. "We don't expect that. We'll find a way."

"We have a huge courtyard out the back of the Scone," Jared offered. "We've used it for fundraising concerts for local schools. The space works a treat, with a firmly secured gazebo in case it rains."

"Your sister won't mind?" Kaci asked.

"I'm sure she won't." Jared's mind raced with ideas. "When the school did their concert, we didn't charge them a hire charge, but still made enough in food and drink to make it worth our while." The Scone was freehold, so they had a bit more freedom to do that kind of thing.

"I could contact some of our regular venues and see if they're interested in hosting us." Rachel started making notes. "Leave it with me." She grinned. "Go Flightless!"

"Go Flightless!"

Owen flopped down on the sofa once Rachel and Kaci had left. He'd enjoyed lunch, yet it now felt heavy on his stomach. He needed to move, to think. He'd offered to help Jared with the dishes, but Gran had told him to take some time out.

He suspected she wanted to talk to Jared in private, which was fair enough considering he'd had her ear earlier that morning.

"I'm off to my knitting group." Gran popped her head around the corner. "I'll be a couple of hours. The spare key is hanging in the usual spot, so don't feel like you have to spend the afternoon here." She smiled. "If you and Jared want to extend your visit a bit before heading back into reality, the offer's there too. Let me know when you've decided."

"Thanks, Gran. Enjoy your group." Owen loved that, although Gran was retired, she'd kept active with her interests and continued to be a part of her community.

He leaned back, tucking his legs up under him. A moment later, Kijé jumped up on him and demanded attention. He patted the cat absently, his thoughts wandering, not for the first time, about how different his mum and gran were. While Gran bloomed with what she'd done in life, Mum had never found pleasure in the little things or the stuff that truly mattered.

Or if she did, she kept it to herself. While she got excited about her projects, Owen had never seen a line between her work and everything else.

"You okay staying here a few more days?" Jared placed a steaming cup of coffee in front of Owen and then settled down with tea in one of Gran's many music-themed mugs.

"Yeah, if you are." Owen snuggled into Jared. They'd taken a longer rental on the van to avoid having to rush in getting it back, and to keep their options open. Or at least that's what Rachel had said. Owen suspected she'd probably guessed that he and Jared would want to stay at Gran's for a few days. *If* she and Gran hadn't already planned it ahead of time.

Kijé dug his claws in, showing his displeasure at Owen's movement, and then settled again, draping himself across both of them.

Jared scratched behind the cat's ears and was rewarded by a loud purr. "I had a long chat with Gran. I really like her." He took a sip of tea. "She's practical too and has some good ideas about all this fundraising stuff."

ANNE BARWELL

"I figured she would. Years of experience at that kind of thing and all that." Owen suspected Jared was leading into something and decided to get there first. "What did you talk about? If you don't mind me asking?"

"She's worried about you." Jared put down his tea and brushed his lips against Owen's. "So am I."

"I'm…" Owen sighed, not bothering to pretend. Jared was getting way too good at reading him like a book. "First off, there's no way I'm missing Rocktoberfest. Wow, just wow, but… God, I can't decide what I want with what happens next. Ditching the audition would make life easier all around, but I'd always have that niggle that perhaps I might have made the cut."

"You need to go through with the audition." Jared sounded thoughtful. "I'm thinking an extra couple of days here would be good. You need some time for yourself to sort things through. Or at least I would, in your situation," he added quickly. "Shit, I'm not trying to tell you what to do."

"I wasn't thinking you were." Owen rested his head on Jared's shoulder, a position that had quickly become a favourite for both of them. "I love that you're concerned and trying to figure out a solution. Taking a few days to talk about everything would be great." If he went into the audition with his attention divided, he'd totally screw it up.

"If you want to think rather than talk, I'm happy to give you some space too," Jared offered.

"No, I want you here." Owen smiled. "You're the first partner I've had who I feel has my back no matter what. I love you for that." He kissed the side of Jared's neck. "And a lot more than that, too."

Jared chuckled. "I hope so." He was quiet for a moment. "Would you mind if Gran joins in some of the conversation too?"

"She'll be there with bells on." Owen snorted at the

144

thought of keeping her out, although she would give them privacy if they asked. It didn't seem right not to include her. He'd always talked to her and Grandpa about any of his major life decisions, so it was second nature by now.

"Perhaps we could work on some music while we're here too," Jared suggested. "Something new for Rocktoberfest, perhaps?"

"I'd love that." Owen mentally went through the list of everything he needed to do between now and October. "Shit, there's so much to do. If we don't get started soon, we'll run out of time."

"That was one reason I suggested it, the other being that composing might be a good distraction and a way to unwind." Jared flushed and gave in to Kijé's request for more patting. "Writing music with you feels like magic. I love creating something new and seeing a whisper of an idea grow into a fully formed song."

"That's what I think too, although I don't have those words." Owen picked a spot of dust off Kijé's coat. "I was going to say it's awesome."

"Well, it is that too," Jared said with a straight face. He glanced out of the window. "How do you feel about going for a walk? After being cramped up in the van a lot of yesterday, I could do with stretching my legs for a bit and getting some fresh air."

"Before we settle down and get lost in music?" Owen nodded. The weather was supposed to go to shit over the next few days too. "Yeah, I'd like that too." He finished his coffee and shifted the cat, who meowed his displeasure.

Once they'd retrieved their jackets, Owen handed Jared one of the scarves hanging by the front door. "Gran keeps a swag of these for whoever wants one. If you want a different one, help yourself. She'll expect you to keep it."

"Cool." Jared wrapped it around his neck. "I've never had

a hand-knitted scarf before. Brigit's one attempt at knitting was a disaster."

"Take one for her too, if you like. Gran would love that. She's probably dying to meet your sister." Owen scribbled Gran a note, although they'd probably be back first, and then waited for Jared to exit the house before locking it behind them.

"I'll bring Brigit over one day." Jared pulled a face. "I suspect they'd get on a little too well. Perhaps I should just drop her off and run."

"Good luck with that." Owen laughed. He kicked up some of the leaves on the driveway and watched them catch in the wind. "Anywhere in particular you'd like to go?"

"I figure just head to the end of the street and see where that leads us?" Jared suggested. "I love looking at houses and imagining the people who live there, especially the older style houses in this kind of neighbourhood."

Owen sang a few lines of a popular song about little houses and boxes. "When we were small, Al and I often stayed with Gran and Grandpa when Mum and Dad were busy with work. They'd take us for walks and find fun things for us to do along the way. One time, we counted all the cats we could see. The one with the most won." He looked smug. "I always spotted them first."

"That sounds like a challenge." Jared pointed to Kijé, who was in the window watching them. "One."

"You're on." Owen led them down the street. Two cats ran out in front of him, skidding to a halt when they reached the edge of the berm. "Two." He slipped his hand into Jared's. "We should scrounge some gloves from Gran, too. She's always got some on the go. I think she has a pair to match your scarf."

"I'd love that." Jared squeezed Owen's hand. "Two and

three." He pointed with his free hand to a couple of cats on a fence across the street. "This is fun."

Another few minutes, and no more cats later, Owen broke the comfortable silence between them. "I'm going to hand in my notice to the shop after we get back from the US."

"You said you were thinking about it." Jared adjusted his scarf. The wind was coming up and taking the late afternoon warmth with it. "Are you going to look for something else straight away?"

"They owe me a fair bit of leave, even counting what I'll need in October, and I have enough savings to pay the mortgage for a while." A blur of white and grey raced across the road. "Three."

"Do you want to wait and see what happens with your audition first?"

"I need to leave, whatever the outcome of that." Owen had finally made the decision and he wanted to move on. "I thought about doing it sooner, but having that income for a few more months would help with getting to Rocktoberfest." A ginger cat strolled over and rubbed up against his ankles. "Four." He bent to pat the cat, grinning when he read the name on its collar. "Watch out for this one. He steals shoes, but only one, never a pair. His family has a notice outside their house about it."

Jared laughed. "You're serious? Wow, but he seems so friendly."

"That's to lull you into a false sense of security while he cases the joint or rather your feet." Owen let the cat sniff his shoes. "No, you're not getting these."

The cat eyed them both in patented feline disdain and then wandered off.

"I've been so busy talking about me." Owen felt a pang of

guilt. "What about your future? Any thoughts about Rockto-berfest or beyond?"

"I'm still pinching myself to make sure this is real," Jared admitted. "Rocktoberfest. Wow." He bit his lip. "I feel bad for Lincoln, though. He's going to be disappointed that he was so close to doing this, but not."

"Lincoln is where he is meant to be," Owen said softly. "He'll be disappointed, but I doubt he'll voice it." He hoped like hell that Lincoln and Duncan's relationship worked out and Lincoln had finally found his forever person.

"Yeah, I guess."

A black cat peered at them from behind a bush, but Jared seemed distracted.

"Five," Owen said after a few moments debating whether he should take advantage of the partly hidden cat. "So… after Rocktoberfest? Although staying where you are is a totally valid answer too. If you've found where you want to be, why change it?" He shrugged to lighten his words. "Not everyone dithers about life like I do."

Jared pulled Owen closer and kissed him soundly. His lips felt cold. They'd need to head home soon. "You're not dither-ing. You're choosing your path." He started at the movement behind them, turning when a small tortoiseshell cat jumped over a nearby fence. "Four. And I think I'd like to focus more on the Scone and be around a bit more for Brigit, whether it's on the counter or behind the scenes. The place has room to grow into more than just a café. People, especially teenagers and older folk, need places where they feel safe, and welcome. We have a side room we use for storage that we don't really need. It could be easily turned into something cosy or opened up in summer. There's a fireplace in the corner and French doors that open up into the back of the property."

"The premises used to be an old house, yeah?"

"Yeah. When we bought the building, we expanded the existing kitchen and added another smaller one and a second bathroom upstairs so it could be used as a self-contained flat. We had ideas of renting it out to help pay for everything, but Brigit loved it so much she moved in. A few family friends helped out with labour and it didn't cost as much as we thought." Jared smiled, a wistful expression that reflected in his eyes. "Mum and Dad would have loved the idea of a community space too. I wish they were here to talk to about it."

"You still have family," Owen reminded him. "We're all here for you, and I know your parents are looking down and feeling very proud. You're a good man, Jared." He hesitated. "You won't want to use your savings to get to Rocktoberfest if you've earmarked them for this."

"I'll make it work." Jared shoved his hands in his pocket. "Like you, I'm not giving up this opportunity. If it takes a bit longer for our plans for the Scone, so be it. Rocktoberfest is probably a one-off, and it's in a few months, while the community space is only an idea at present. We hadn't planned to start looking at it seriously until next year."

"A fundraiser concert at the Scone would be a good trial run of the space. We can help you clear it out. Rachel loves that kind of thing. You saw what she did with her garage once she decided it would make a great rehearsal space." Owen hoped Rachel didn't mind that he was volunteering her, although she had enough self-preservation to say no if she couldn't do it.

"The school concerts worked well, but...."

"They already had a guaranteed audience. This won't." Owen stopped walking, a thought hitting him, waves of excitement running through him. "What if we wrote a new song, especially for these fundraising concerts? We have a few regulars who show up to all our performances. I'm sure advertising these events as being the first to hear it would be a drawcard."

"We need a new one for Rocktoberfest too," Jared said slowly, "but we managed that and more for Frays, and that was a shorter time frame. What about your audition, though? That's a lot closer now."

"I'll manage." Owen hooked his arm through Jared's and started walking again. "It's getting cold. What say we head home and get started."

A cat skidded to a halt across their path.

They looked at each other, neither claiming it.

"That one's yours, and then we're even," Owen offered.

"Or yours if you want to win, sweetheart."

Owen shook his head. "I've already won, in all the ways that matter." He initiated the kiss between them this time. "Actually… Gran's going to be out for a while longer. We'll have the house to ourselves for at least another hour. My old bed is very comfortable, and…."

"Yes. Always yes." Jared's gaze heated in desire. "You're the only prize I need, and I want to show you how much."

"Love you." Owen let go of Jared. "Race you. First one home gets to undress the other."

Jared grinned. "You're on."

CHAPTER FOURTEEN

Owen finished the final note of the Bach sonata and lowered his violin. The four members of the Oriolidae Quartet glanced at each other, smiled, and then scribbled notes before their current second violinist spoke.

"Very impressive." Susie Dayton was taking over as first violin, leaving her current position as second for whomever impressed them enough to win the role. "What made you choose this particular piece?"

"I like the different moods of each movement." Owen had expected this question and rehearsed his answer until it rolled off his tongue when his mind was too panicked to string words together. "I also thought the final movement, in particular, would showcase my skill." His response was greeted by silence, and he blurted out before he could stop himself, "and my cat's name is Bach."

Shit, that sounded lame. Owen cursed his response, but couldn't take it back now.

To his surprise, their cellist, Jake Costello, laughed. "I love that, and having a sense of humour is definitely something we're looking for. Rehearsals, especially leading up to a performance, can get very intense. Humour is a necessary survival skill."

"Most definitely, although I must warn you that some of Jake's jokes are particularly bad." Avril Westin, their retiring violinist, spoke with affection. This group was close and from what Owen had read and already observed, had a strong family vibe.

"Hey," Jake protested, although he grinned. "Avril's sad she's going to miss them after all these years together."

"We're not only looking for a skilled violinist but someone who will fit in personality and share our goals." Sefa Fong had played viola with them for the last five years and was the closest to Owen in age.

Susie and Jake were both in their mid-forties, although there wasn't a lot of personal information about them online, only the biographic spiel attached to the quartet's website. Owen didn't blame them. Being in the spotlight wasn't easy, although he'd never dealt with it on the same scale, and only in short bursts with Flightless.

Avril had originally been Susie's music teacher and formed the quartet with an old friend, whom Sefa had taken over from.

"I've played in an orchestra for the past ten years." Owen repeated the information he'd already given them.

"Your concert master speaks highly of you." Avril smiled. "You've mainly played first violin, and this position is for second."

"I realise that," Owen assured her, "and the difference between the two. I played second in my first orchestra in high school...." He hesitated and then grew silent.

"And?" Susie prompted.

"I've played in another... group... since high school, and

often other instruments take the limelight, and the rest of us support them with our own parts."

"I love classical music, but sometimes I need a change of palate." Susie seemed pleased with his answer. "It's not widely known, and definitely not on our website, but I play fiddle for a Scottish music band when their usual fiddler isn't available."

"I've been to a few of their gigs. They're definitely worth checking out." Sefa grinned. "I met my girlfriend at one of them."

"Wow, that's cool." Owen felt a glimmer of hope. If Susie was able to find time to play in a band, maybe he wouldn't need to completely give up Flightless.

"You should come to a concert sometime." Susie spoke in a low voice to Avril, who nodded, and then continued. "You've more than shown us your skill as a solo performance. We sent you the music for two quartet pieces, but today, we'll play only one." She turned to Sefa and Jake. "My vote's for Mendelsohn, although I'm open to Beethoven too."

"Mendelsohn works for me," Jake said.

"Same." Sefa retrieved his viola and indicated the chair to his left. "This will work better if you take Susie's spot, Owen, and she can be Avril."

"I don't think anyone can be Avril." Susie chuckled, but something in her voice sounded strained.

Was she as nervous about taking over from Avril as Owen was about his audition? Owen caught the edge of his stand and sent his sheet music flying.

"Shit, sorry." His face heated, and he gathered his music from the floor. Luckily, he'd secured it in a folder, so he wasn't picking up individual pieces of paper.

"That's usually my trick." Jake caught Owen's eye and winked. "I think you'll fit in here well."

Avril cleared her throat.

"If you get the gig, of course," Jake added quickly. "You're our last audition, but we still need to make a decision."

Susie played an A and waited for them to tune to her violin. Once everyone indicated they were ready, she led them into the piece.

Owen's nervousness dissolved once the music took over. Susie, Safa, and Jake's length of time playing together showed immediately, but Owen found it easy to support each of their instruments in turn and become the glue holding their performance together while letting each instrument shine in their time in the limelight.

The piece finished too soon, and Owen sat back in his chair, surprised by how much he wanted to be a part of this. Playing with Flightless definitely filled a hole in his soul, but so did this.

Panic rushed through him at the thought of having to choose. His breathing sped up, and the room spun. He pushed back his chair but couldn't bring himself to stand.

Fuck, what was he going to do?

An image of Jared filled his mind, his eyes crinkled in a warm smile. Whatever Owen decided would be okay.

But he didn't want to decide. He'd hoped playing with the quartet would put his desire to rest, or he'd never get this far in the audition. His mum had told him that they'd only ask him to play the second violin part for one of these pieces if they were seriously considering him for the role.

"Hey, it's okay." Susie knelt by him, concern in her eyes. "What's wrong? This isn't performance anxiety. Not with the way you played so confidently before."

Owen bit his lip. He needed to come clean. "I'm sorry. I haven't been completely honest with you…" He took a deep breath. "At the very least, if you still want me, I can't start in

October anyway. I have a gig in the US, and I've already promised I'm in for it."

"A gig in the US?" Jake whistled. "In October?" Excitement danced across his face. "Hang on a moment. I thought your name seemed familiar but then presumed it was because of your mum. You're Owen Stanton from Flightless, yeah?"

"Yeah. That's me." Owen was surprised Jake had heard of them. "My band is playing at Rocktoberfest this year."

"Shit, man, that's way cool." Sufa high-fived him.

Avril looked puzzled. "Rocktoberfest?"

"It's a huge annual rock concert in Arizona," Sufa explained. "Bands from all over the world take part. It's a big deal to get an invite." His tone grew serious. "And one you totally can't turn down."

"Definitely not." Susie agreed and then frowned. "So… what are your plans if we want you, after Rocktoberfest, of course."

"My decision to retire in October isn't set in concrete," Avril said. "I'm happy to stay a bit longer, as long as Owen's back for rehearsals for our end-of-year concert in December."

"I'd definitely be back for that if you want me." Owen sighed. "I really want to play with you, but I'm torn. I'm not sure I can choose between this and the band. I love classical music, and playing with you just now was amazing, but Flightless has been a part of my life for a long time." He glanced at Sufa. "It's also how I met my boyfriend."

Susie frowned. "Why do you think you have to choose?"

"Mum…." Owen trailed off. His mother had strongly implied that he couldn't have both and that it was time to put this silly rock band business behind him. Her words, not his.

"I'll be having words with your mother." Avril pursed her lips. "Lindsey excels at finding and nurturing musical talent, but she's a little tunnel-visioned. Many professional musicians have other gigs. Susie loves Scottish music, Jake conducts a couple of school choirs, Sufa teaches music and plays bass guitar in a band on the weekend, and I've conducted a few local orchestras in my time."

"Sufa plays in a band?" Owen couldn't believe what he was hearing. "So... you wouldn't have any issues if I did both?"

"Of course not, as long as we were able to sit down at the beginning of each year and make sure our schedules didn't clash." Susie squeezed Owen's shoulder. "As Jake said, we still need to make a decision, so I can't tell you the outcome of your audition, although you're one of our top three contenders for the role."

"Wow, thank you." For the first time in months, a heaviness lifted from Owen's soul, the burden having grown worse the closer he'd been to this audition. "Thank you for your time and consideration."

"Thank you for auditioning." Avril smiled. "I promise we won't keep you in suspense for too long."

∽

"How are our finances looking?" Jared slipped into the seat next to Rachel, hoping he wasn't reading her demeanour correctly.

"We're still quite a bit short," Rachel confirmed.

The Scone was their last venue for their fundraising gigs. The response so far had been great, but not quite enough. Getting to the US from New Zealand wasn't cheap, and Clay's hope of contributing more towards his share had hit a huge pothole quite literally when he'd had to replace his money pit of a car.

"Maybe we'll get some extras through the door this afternoon."

The Scone was booked to capacity, but with the weather in their favour, they could find room for last-minute door sales and seat them on the grass outside around the edges of the gazebo.

"That will help, but..." Rachel sighed. "I guess I could take out a loan if it came down to it. I'm sure Rocktoberfest will put the band on the rock music map, so I'd be able to pay it back quickly."

"And what if you can't?" Jared hated to pour cold water on her idea, but he remembered the early days of The Scone all too well when he and Brigit had worried that they were on the road to bankruptcy. "If we don't make up the difference today, we'll *all* take out loans. Share and share alike. You shouldn't have to carry the burden for this."

"It's not a burden..." Rachel shook her head. "Let's just see what happens today, okay? Promise me you won't mention this to anyone else yet." She paused. "Except Owen, of course. I figure what you know, he needs to."

"Sure." Jared would wait until their planned finance meeting the following night before mentioning anything to anyone else. A miracle could happen between this and then, right? He took Rachel's hand in his and squeezed it. "We'll get to Rocktoberfest one way or another, you'll see."

Brigit waved to him from behind the counter.

"Yeah, we will," Rachel said. "I'm not doubting the will, just the how. Go see what Brigit wants, and thank her again for her generosity."

"She's thrilled to be a part of what she's calling our road to Rocktoberfest." Jared sprinted over to Brigit. "How's it going? Need any help?"

Everything was about ready to go. Phil and Tyler were helping Kaci set up the chairs, and Clay was deep in conversation with Father Elard, who had turned up early to take over the door sales. He'd also offered to help out behind the bar to serve drinks to those who wanted them.

Considering Duncan had donated several cartons of Frays' wine, Elard would be in for a busy evening. The priest had also sent word out through his large network of friends and patrons about the concert, and sold a few tickets.

"I think we have enough." Brigit had outdone herself and made several batches of strawberry scones in honour of the occasion. "Gran's offered to help out when she arrives, although there isn't much that needs doing."

"You've got this, boss." Julie had offered to work the afternoon for free, donating what would have been overtime for her.

"*We've* got this." Brigit grinned, and Julie flushed, then smiled a sweet smile, and met Brigit's gaze. "I'm taking you out for dinner tonight after we're done. You've been a rock through all of this."

"My pleasure." Julie disappeared out the back into the kitchen.

Okaay… Jared had been away from the Scone for too long. He was seriously missing something. "So, you and Julie?" he asked as soon as Julie was out of earshot.

Brigit looked smug. "I wondered how long it would take you to notice. We've been taking it slow, and it's still very new." She held up a hand before Jared could warn her about complications. "Don't worry, we have all that employer/employee stuff sorted. Around the time we realised how we felt, Julie decided she wanted to finish her graphics degree. She's handing in her notice once that's sorted…."

"You're going to need a new barista."

"I hope I already have one." Brigit gave him a pointed look, and then her expression softened. "You've been talking about how you're over all the travelling you're doing. The

Scone is both of ours and always has been. I was thinking that perhaps it's time for you to be more hands-on. If you're okay with doing that, I already have someone interested in taking on a casual role for when you're away on gigs and in the States in October."

"You've got all this sorted." Jared felt a weight lift. "I'd been trying to figure out how to broach the subject but figured you had enough on your plate with today."

"I've only sorted up to a point. I started interviewing to save time, but I wouldn't hire anyone without your approval first." Brigit gave him a hug. "And you can talk to me anytime. When have I ever been too busy to listen?"

"Never," Jared admitted. "I'm really happy for you and Julie." He'd always liked her. "Who do you have in mind for the casual role? Anyone I know?"

"Claire Weatherby."

"Ah." Jared nodded his approval. He'd worked with Claire before. She was capable, good-tempered, and proactive. "You have been busy."

"So have you, so I didn't want to bother you with this until you were ready." Brigit looked up when the café door opened, and smiled. "Owen's made good time." She leaned in. "This is going to be great, Jared. You and Flightless are going to rock it, and everything will turn out okay, I promise."

"Thanks." Jared greeted Owen with a kiss on his cheek. "Hi, Gran. We're all happy you're here."

"Like anything was going to keep me away." Gran gave Jared a hug. "I'm going to hang up my coat and see what Brigit needs me to do. Remember to have fun, boys. This is going to be a great afternoon." She caught up with Brigit, the two of them chatting amicably as they walked together into the kitchen.

"Those two get on a little too well," Owen said. "Sometimes I wonder if I should be worried about that."

"Only sometimes?" Jared teased.

"I was playing it down." Owen chuckled. He'd been sleeping better since discovering he could have both Flightless and Oriolidae, and lost the shadows under his eyes. However, the longer he waited for news from the quartet, the less certain he became that they'd chosen him for the role. "Seriously though, I'm happy that Gran has found a kindred spirit in Brigit."

"They have a little too much in common." Jared rolled his eyes in tandem with Owen, and they both laughed.

"Like their determination to make sure we get our HEA?" Owen used the term Brigit loved to bandy around.

"News flash, sweetheart." Jared pulled Owen into his arms and kissed him. "I already have."

"Get a room, you two." Kaci wolf-whistled, a huge grin on her face. "We'll be opening the doors soon, and we want people to be focused on the main event."

"You mean we're not?" Owen mock pouted then pretended to be offended when Kaci rolled her eyes.

"In your dreams." Kaci peered out the window. "It's too quiet out there. I thought we'd at least have something of a queue by now."

"People aren't going to buy tickets and then not turn up," Jared reassured her, "and besides, they've already paid for them."

"I need to tune." Owen indicated the violin case in his free hand, "and I could do with a coffee, if that's okay."

"My keyboard's already set up. I'll grab you a coffee and meet you there." Jared wished for a moment that he drank coffee as it might settle his nerves. No matter how many times he played, he couldn't shake his pre-performance jitters.

"I'll be waiting." Owen disappeared into the room they were using to store their gear, leaving Jared alone with Kaci.

"Still nothing from Oriolidae?" she asked.

"Not as far as I know." Jared figured that meant no news, and hopefully, that was a good thing. "I'm sure he aced the audition. What he said sounded positive."

"He needs to know sooner rather than later." Kaci leaned in and gave Jared a chaste peck on the cheek.

"What's that for?" Jared frowned. Kaci was touchy-feely with Owen and Clay, but not with him. They didn't have the same history.

"That's a thank you. You're good for Owen. He's relaxed and more himself since you guys got together." She glanced around and then lowered her voice. "And I don't mean just about the Oriolidae thing. He's spent far too much of his life tying himself up in knots, trying to please his mum." Her nose crinkled. "And I'm not sure anything he did would ever do that."

"Unless he ditched Flightless and focused solely on his classical career." Jared hadn't voiced his disgust to Owen about how Lindsey had used the audition to force Owen to make a choice he didn't have to.

"Good thing that's not happening, yeah?" Kaci scanned the room and smiled when her gaze settled on Rachel. "I'm going to get my girl a cuppa. She's been working way too hard the last few weeks worrying about getting everything to balance and show the result she wants."

"She told you?"

"Duh. We don't keep secrets, any more than you and Owen do."

"That's good." Jared hesitated. "I don't suppose you could make a pot, so I could grab a cuppa too."

"No problem. Although I suspect your gran's already onto it." Kaci took off towards Rachel, leaving Jared to grab Owen's coffee.

By the time he reached the kitchen, a cup of coffee sat on

the counter, along with a pot of freshly brewed tea. He called out his thanks to Gran, poured the tea, and went to catch up with Owen.

"Almost done here." Owen ran his bow over his A string and then fiddled with the tuning peg. "And totally needing that coffee." One more tweak of the peg, and he returned his violin to its case. "There's always one string more stubborn than the rest." He took the cup of coffee, sniffed appreciatively, and sat on the floor with his back against the wall. "Smells divine."

"Your gran's brew." Jared joined Owen and intertwined the fingers on their free hands. Finding some time together with a decent brew had become one of their pre-concert routines. Usually, that meant a couple of thermoses in a corner of a green room, but today's location provided the luxury of freshly made in a crockery mug. "Both of them."

"I figured." Owen sipped his coffee. "This sounds crazy, but this feels like the end of an era and the beginning of a new adventure for the band. Frays was great, and I've enjoyed all these concerts, but wow... I still can't get my head around being on stage at Rocktoberfest."

"You'll have to prop me up to get me on stage," Jared joked. He stroked Owen's thumb, the motion calming. "You'd think I'd be used to this by now, but I'm totally not."

"You don't show it once we start playing." Owen brought their joined hands up to his mouth and kissed Jared's fingers. "When I first started playing in public, I felt like puking. I was so nervous. I didn't think I'd ever make it through the performance."

"What happened?" Jared swallowed a mouthful of tea and then rested his head on Owen's shoulder.

"Gran told me that most of the people listening couldn't do what I could, and the only opinion that mattered was my own. Focus on the music and play the concert for one person. That's what I've done ever since."

"That's why you told me to focus on you at Frays."

"Yeah." Owen kissed Jared softly, tasting of coffee and passion. "And instead of thinking about last night, when we were too tired to do anything, that's a promise for later." He put down his cup. "A prelude to our very own symphony, sweetheart."

CHAPTER FIFTEEN

Owen glanced around the audience, taking care to make eye contact with those in the first row. They'd had some extras turn up, and a few fans who had supported them by coming to every concert.

Clay stepped up to the mic. "Thanks for coming again to support us on our road to Rocktoberfest. We're excited to be heading over to the States to play at such a huge event." He paused and smiled. "But, however far we go, we'll always have a place in our heart for those of you who have been cheerleading us from the beginning, and also our new friends we've met during this series of fundraising concerts."

The crowd clapped, and a group at the back whistled their appreciation.

"We figured we'd do something special with this last concert." Clay's smile morphed into a grin. "This first performance of a new song is for our fans. For you." He stood back and handed the mic to Owen.

Owen swallowed to quell the butterflies in his stomach. He might not be as nervous as Jared before a concert, but he felt more at ease playing his violin. "Clouds surround me," he sang, with Phil accompanying him on guitar. "Growing darker. Overwhelming." He turned to Jared, and they shared a smile. "I'm looking for light, a glimpse of sunlight to give me hope during darker days."

Tyler joined Phil, the bass and guitar weaving melody and chords together, the key changing from minor to major when Jared stood and joined Owen at the mic.

"Sweetheart, you're my sunshine, my break in the storm," Jared sang. "Let me be that for you."

"My break in the storm," they repeated together, in harmony.

Kaci joined in on drums, adding a heartbeat to the music. Clay picked up his guitar and strummed chords in unison with Tyler for the bridge until Tyler broke off and played the melody line on his guitar.

Owen followed Jared to his keyboard and retrieved his violin. They repeated the melody line, this time on their instruments rather than singing.

Clay stepped up to the mike, singing and playing. "Sunshine, on a cloudy day. Stillness in the eye of life's storms, calm amongst the winds of change."

"My sunshine, my break in the storm," they all sang together.

Owen risked a look at the audience, relief rushing through him. They seemed to like it, shit he *hoped* they did.

Kaci launched into the verse. "You're my sunshine, always have been, forever us. Need the dark sometimes to know the light. All things pass with time. I want to pass my time with you." Her voice soared with the high notes, her tone pure and clear. Rachel, sitting in the front row, wiped at her eyes.

Another repeat of the chorus, and then the instruments bowed out one by one, with Jared, and then Owen finishing playing last.

"Sweetheart, you're my break in the storm," Jared sang.

"And you're my sunshine," Owen sang in harmony. "My light in darker days."

Jared stopped singing and smiled.

"My light in darker days," Owen repeated solo, twice, his voice slowing and then fading away.

The audience erupted into applause, several of them standing to clap. The band put down their instruments, linked arms, and took a bow.

"Go Flightless!" yelled Rachel.

"Go Flightless!" someone from the audience joined in.

The band bowed again and then left the stage.

"Wow," Kaci said. "They really loved that last song."

"Great idea to have a first performance of it here." Brigit came up to them. "Fabulous show. Do you mind if I steal your microphone now you're not using it?"

"Of course." Clay stood back to let her pass. "And thanks again for hosting us. This is a wonderful venue. We'll have to come back here, if you'll have us."

"Of course." Brigit's mouth twitched. "Although I'll have to talk to my business partner about that."

"Dork." Jared grinned.

"You did?" Owen asked.

"Yeah. We talked before. It's all sorted." Jared kissed Owen, not caring who was watching. "I'll be focusing on the Scone going forward and Flightless, of course." He whispered in Owen's ear. "And you, sweetheart. That was some prelude."

Owen wrapped his arm around Jared's waist.

Brigit tapped the microphone. "Is this thing on?" It screeched in affirmation, and she grimaced. "Sorry, it's my brother who knows this stuff, not me."

"Stand back from it a bit," Jared yelled. "You're a natural."

The audience chuckled, especially when Brigit replied with a rude gesture to Jared.

"Thanks, little bro." Brigit cleared her throat. "But anyway... I want to add my thanks for the turnout today. We're thrilled to be hosting Flightless, a band going places." She lowered her voice like she was sharing a secret. "And I'm not just saying that because my brother's in it."

Owen leaned into Jared, enjoying the banter. He loved the closeness between the siblings and how Brigit had welcomed him so quickly into her family. A movement caught his eye at the back of the room.

Shit, everyone from Oriolidae was here. Hopefully, they had news for him. All this waiting was way too stressful. Or had they come out of curiosity to hear the concert?

"Don't forget to help yourselves to the after-concert refreshments. We have a selection of baked goods, fresh from our kitchen, great wine from Frays Vineyard, and also juice, tea, and coffee."

Elard stood watching her from the sidelines while speaking quietly to a man who Owen recognised as one of his regulars from Arpeggios. He and his partner often came into the shop to look through sheet music. Owen glanced back at Brigit, and when he looked for Elard again, he was alone and heading up onto the stage. He whispered something to Brigit, who grinned and pulled him into a hug.

"Fabulous news from Father Elard!" She sounded excited. "We've just received a huge donation to the Rocktoberfest fund! The person wants to remain anonymous, but today has been a huge success, and thanks to all of you and everyone who has supported the band, it looks like we've achieved our goal."

"Woot!" Gran yelled from the back of the café. "Go Flightless!"

"Wow, that's so cool." Jared could hardly contain his excitement, and relief. He'd been mentally going over the logistics of getting a loan to make up the shortfall but had hoped that none of them would have to.

Tyler kissed Phil, the two of them melting into each other's arms. "Now we just have to decide whether to get married before or afterwards."

"You're getting married?" Kaci yelled, then flushed. "Oops, sorry, I hope that wasn't meant to be a secret."

"Bit late for that now." Phil grinned and pulled her into a hug. "We've been waiting in case we needed the money for Rocktoberfest."

"Shit, guys, I didn't know you were putting your wedding on hold!" Owen looked shocked.

"Eh, a few more months wouldn't have hurt." Tyler shrugged. "We've moved in together already." He glanced around. "I wish we could say thanks to whoever provided that last donation."

"Anonymous for a reason," Elard murmured when he reached them. "And congratulations, you two. If you need a priest, I'd be delighted to officiate."

"Thanks, but not Catholic, Father," Tyler said.

Elard grinned. "You don't need to be. The last wedding I officiated at wasn't." He gave them all a wave. "I need to catch up with a few people. Wonderful concert. Your trip is very well deserved."

He wandered off before anyone could comment.

Duncan chuckled behind them. "Don't worry. He does that a lot. Sometimes I think he likes to wander in and out of other people's lives, sprinkling goodwill as he goes."

"I loved that last song," Lincoln added. "You've got yourselves a winning songwriting combination there." He ducked his head. "Lyrics were never my thing. I knew Jared and Owen would hit it off in more ways than one."

"Thanks for sending him to me... to us." Owen glanced at Jared and then back at Lincoln. "We do still miss playing with you, you know."

"Yeah, me too." Lincoln smiled. "I'll find where I'm meant to be when it's the right time, I'm sure."

Duncan tugged at him. "I've just seen some friends I want you to meet." He looked apologetic. "Sorry, I'll bring him back later, promise."

"Speaking of people..." Owen suddenly seemed nervous. "I need to go talk to someone, too."

Something about him sparked Jared's protective side. "Do you need me to come with you?"

"Yeah. I'd like that, thanks." Owen slipped his hand into Jared's. "Catch you later, okay?"

"Sure." Kaci raised an eyebrow. "Everything okay?"

"I hope so." Owen's hand felt clammy in Jared's.

"What's up?" Jared asked as soon as they were out of earshot.

"Oriolidae are here," Owen blurted out. "I saw them in the audience during the last song. I'm not sure whether they're still here or...."

"Shit. Do you want to talk to them alone?" Jared would do whatever Owen needed. "Do you think you should talk to them?"

Surely, they wouldn't have come here only to disappear and not say anything. From the way Owen had described them, they all seemed decent.

Avril Westin strode towards Owen, obviously seeking him out. Jared recognised her from the quartet's website. Not that he'd read everything he could about them.

Much.

"Owen," she said with a huge smile. "I hadn't realised how good your band was. You're truly remarkable."

"Thanks, and for coming to support us today. It means a

lot." Owen tightened his grip on Jared's hand. "This is my boyfriend, Jared Murphy. Jared, Avril Westin, currently first violinist of Oriolidae."

"It's a pleasure to meet you, Jared." Avril studied him for a moment. "You and Owen write a lot of band's songs, yes?"

"Yes. Owen's a talented musician." Jared shrugged. "I write the lyrics. The rest is all his."

"It's both of us," Owen corrected him. He cleared his throat but said nothing. "I don't suppose you…."

"We've kept you waiting, and I'm sorry about that," Avril said. "Unfortunately, Susie had that nasty flu bug that's going around, and we needed to give her time to recover. The three violinists we had to choose between were all very talented, and our decision wasn't an easy one."

Here it comes. Oh God, I'm so sorry, sweetheart.

"I understand," Owen responded with an obviously forced smile that didn't meet his eyes. "I hope…."

"The position is yours if you want it." Avril indicated the now empty stage. "Although after that performance, we'd totally understand if you'd prefer to focus on Flightless, and withdraw your application."

"Fuck, no." Owen turned bright red. "Sorry, I didn't mean to swear. I don't… I'd love to play with you. Thank you." He hesitated. "As long as it's still okay for me to do both."

"Of course." Avril's smile widened. "We're very pleased to welcome you to our Oriolidae family." She met Jared's gaze. "Both of you. Family is very important to us, and we wouldn't be where we are today without the support of our loved ones. You'll have to introduce me to the rest of Flightless very soon, too, but in the meantime, could you point me in the direction of your manager. Rachel, isn't it? I want to exchange contact information with her so we can work out scheduling for when you get back from the States."

"Sure." Owen glanced behind Avril and grimaced. "And there's Mum approaching. Right on cue."

"She doesn't know." Avril looked smug. "We figured you'd like that honour."

"Do you want to introduce Avril and Rachel?" Jared suggested. "I'll head off your mum until you get back."

"Thanks." Owen kissed Jared's cheek. "Give me a few minutes to digest all this first if you can," he whispered.

"Of course." Jared took a step forward and intercepted Lindsey before she could reach Owen. "Lindsey!" He plastered on his biggest fake smile. "We're so glad you were able to make it today to support the band. Isn't it exciting? We're going to Rocktoberfest!"

～

By the time Owen left Avril and Rachel and headed back towards Jared, the café was buzzing with pockets of conversation. The rest of the band chatted with fans. Susie and Jake from Oriolidae were deep in conversation with Gran, and Sefa and Clay laughed over a shared joke.

The warmth spreading through him at the thought that his new and existing families were already getting along didn't quell Owen's anxiety at the upcoming conversation with his mum.

Brigit caught his arm when he walked by. "If you need some privacy, you're welcome to take her upstairs."

"Thanks." Owen guessed she'd caught some of the conversation between his mum and Jared. "I'll do that."

"I can send up some coffee in a few if you'd like, in case you want the cavalry by then."

"Sounds brilliant." Owen kissed her cheek. "You're like the sister I never had. You know that, right?"

She laughed. "Totally. And you're definitely my number

two brother." Brigit hesitated before continuing. Owen had told her about his history with his mum a few weeks ago, although he hadn't intended to. Like her brother, she was easy to talk to. "You've got this, and we've got you."

"Thanks." Owen straightened and wished things were that easy. He managed a smile by the time he reached Jared.

"Hey, sweetheart." Jared greeted him with a kiss. "Your mum loved the concert. She's been singing your praises."

"Well done on reaching your goal," Lindsey said. "Rockto-berfest will be a great send-off for you." She glanced over at Avril, who was still in conversation with Rachel. "I'm presuming she's come to share good news. They'd be crazy to turn down someone with your talent."

"About that…" Owen glanced at Jared. "We need to talk, Mum, and in private. Brigit has kindly offered us the use of the upstairs flat."

"Oh." Lindsey's expression dropped. "I'm so sorry, Owen. I really thought…."

"I'll be here when you need me," Jared added. They'd already agreed if Lindsey showed up, Owen would talk to her privately. "Oh look, there's your dad. I'll go snag him a strawberry scone before they all disappear." He took off in the direction of Owen's dad, clearing the way for Owen and his mum to have their conversation.

Owen led his mum up the stairs. Sun streamed through the French doors that opened onto the balcony that wrapped around the top floor of the house. He indicated one of the overstuffed comfortable chairs in the small living room and then took a seat opposite.

"Avril's offered me the position at Oriolidae," he said quickly to put her out of misery about that at least. "I'll be joining them once we get back from Rocktoberfest."

"Oh, that's great news. I'm so proud of you." Lindsey beamed. "If you need me to help organis—"

"Thanks, but that's all under control. Avril and Rachel are going to sort out schedules and all that."

"I don't understand." Lindsey frowned. "What has Rachel got to do with any of it? You're leaving that band for a classical career like you always wanted to."

"Like *you* always wanted me to," Owen corrected her. "I love classical music, and that's down to you, which I appreciate, but Flightless…" He smiled, thinking of today's performance. "Flightless gives me something classical music doesn't, and vice versa. I need both to feel whole."

"Well, you can't have both." Lindsey pursed her lips.

"Well, *actually*, I can." Owen took a deep breath and reminded himself to stay strong. "When I went for my audition, I was upfront with them and told them about Flightless. I've been tying myself up in knots, thinking I had to choose. I don't. I can do both, as long as our schedules don't clash."

"You can't play for both and continue to work at the shop." Lindsey bit her lip, worry creasing her face. "You'll burn out. I've seen it before with someone taking on too much. I don't want that to happen to you."

"I'm handing in my notice at the shop," Owen reassured her. "I loved Arpeggios when I first started, but the admin side not so much. Oriolidae gives me the financial cushion I need. I'm also leaving the orchestra so I don't stretch myself too far." He didn't mention that he'd planned to leave Arpeggios anyway. "And if Flightless make it big after Rocktoberfest, that's great, but if we don't, well, I'll make it work. Jared and I will make it work."

Lindsey grew quiet. She got up and started to pace, turning her back on Owen. Her shoulders began to shake.

"Mum?" Owen got up and drew her into a hug. "It's okay. I'll be okay. Promise."

"I wanted the world for you." Lindsey met his gaze, tears in her eyes. "And in my determination to do so, I nearly took it away from you. I never… I couldn't do both, so I thought you wouldn't be able to either. I… you've been struggling, and I was too full of what I wanted to notice. Forgive me?"

"You're my mum, and I love you. That will never change." Owen had never heard such emotion from her before. "And what do you mean you couldn't do both?"

Lindsey wiped her eyes. "I used to play violin a very long time ago." She held up her hand to stop him from interrupting when he failed to hide his surprise. "I wasn't as good as you were, and I had to practice a lot, and I mean *a lot*, to be anywhere halfway decent. When I found what I thought was my calling to help nurture talent in others and find the opportunities they deserved, it ate into my practice time. The more successful that role became, the less I played, until one day I stopped and never picked my violin up again."

"I didn't know." Owen couldn't imagine what it would be like to have to stop playing altogether. "Oh, Mum, I'm so sorry."

"How could you know?" Lindsey's smile looked strained. "I took all the photos down at your Gran and Grandpa's and asked them not to tell you."

"Why?"

"I didn't want to ruin your expectations before you'd even started. Everything I've done hasn't been about me."

"Well, maybe that needs to change." Owen hated seeing his mum upset, but a part of him was relieved to finally see a more human side of her. "Does Dad know?"

Lindsey snorted. "Of course not. I stopped playing a few years before we met." Her voice softened. "He would have encouraged me to follow what I loved, but by that stage, my path was clear. I'd never be a great performer. It made more sense to put it behind me and move forward."

"Sometimes the right road isn't the one you think it is," Gran said from behind them, carrying a tray of tea and scones. "Jared sent me. He thought you might need this by now." She shook her head. "Music isn't only about performing and being brilliant, you know. Enjoyment is a big part of it, too. Picking a tune, note by note on the piano, can touch you as much as getting up on stage and playing with a band. Or a quartet."

"I've been an idiot, Mum," Lindsey said.

"We're all guilty of that from time to time, dear." Gran put down the tray and opened her arms. "You've been heading for this moment for a while now. You're burning out and not taking care of your soul." She glanced at Owen. "I won't be making the mistake of standing back again. You try any of this shit, and I won't hesitate to call you on it."

"If Jared doesn't do it first," Owen said.

"That boy's good for you." Lindsey lifted her head and smiled, a genuine expression this time. "I'm sorry I've been distant. I was scared that if I let go, everything would let rip. I'm proud of everything you've done and all your decisions."

"Thanks." Owen had waited far too long to hear his mum tell him that, and know she meant it. "I know what it's like to get sucked into the life you think you want."

"You two are a little alike sometimes." Gran poured the tea. "I'm proud of both of you, and that needs saying too." She smiled. "The tea's not for me, by the way. Jared's waiting downstairs for you, Owen, and... Howard's on his way up. I hope that's okay. He guessed something was going down, and he's not been happy waiting in the wings."

"That's very much okay." Lindsey gave Gran a hug. "You can stay if you want. Things are going to be different going forward."

"Oh, I know, and this isn't my time." Gran chuckled. "How do you think I know about the dangers of this kind of thing? You're very much like your dad, Lindsey. We used to argue about how much he pushed himself. At one point, I thought I'd said too much, but in the end, our marriage was stronger for it."

"I'm going to find Jared." Owen sensed his mum and grandmother needed a few minutes on their own. He kissed both of their foreheads in turn. "Love you."

His dad was waiting at the foot of the stairs. "Safe to go up yet?"

"Yeah, in a few, I think." Owen was surprised when Howard pulled him into a hug. "What's that for?"

"For your brilliant performance today, and I believe congratulations are also in order." Howard grinned. "I'm proud of you, son. And for finding the courage to talk to your mum, which is something I should have done way before things got this far."

Owen shrugged. "Hindsight and all that. It's fine."

"Make sure you and Jared come around for dinner soon before you head off overseas." Howard let go of Owen and headed up the stairs.

"All okay?" Jared looked Owen up and down and then relaxed.

"Yeah. I think it finally is. Or will be."

CHAPTER SIXTEEN

"Boy, it's hot." Owen chugged more water. He couldn't wait to get out of the bus they'd hired, despite it having air-con.

"Remember to keep hydrated," Rachel reminded him. "None of you have been in a desert before, and the heat is going to hit you hard."

"At least it's dry heat and not humid," Kaci added. "Although I bet the locals will laugh at what we think is hot."

"Yeah, there's that." Jared peered out the window at the makeshift city ahead. "Whoa, this place is big. What I envisioned and reality aren't even on the same scale."

Black Rock City stretched out in front of them for miles, its population already way bigger than everyone in New Zealand several times over, including the sheep. A mix of vans, buses, tents, and yurts stretched out into the distance, further than Owen could see.

Their driver pulled over and grinned. "This isn't the first time I've seen this, and I'm still in awe. You guys are going to love it, but as Rachel said, make sure you keep drinking. Management is providing free water, so take advantage of it."

Hiring Brett had been a unanimous decision no one regretted. Apart from Clay, who had spent a year in the US as part of his OE—overseas experience—after he left uni, they all felt like they'd stepped into another world, driving on the other side of the road, aside.

"I'm relieved we're not playing until Friday." Owen yawned. He'd tried to sleep on the flight over, but the mix of excitement and not wanting to miss anything had resulted in a succession of catnaps.

"One fifteen-hour flight was enough for me for a few days," Jared said. "Stop yawning. You're contagious." He seemed more alert than Owen, although that wouldn't take much. "I wish we'd had longer in LA, though."

"I didn't think adding another ten hours to our trip was a great idea," Rachel pointed out. "Plenty of time to unwind by exploring it on the way home."

"This place is amazing." Kaci looked out the window when Brett started driving again. "And oh, my God, I can't believe we're going to be playing in the slot before Grindstone."

"I know, right?" Phil said. "Wow."

"I fully intended to stick around afterwards to watch them perform." Clay let out a sigh.

"Good thing we'll be done and our nerves out of the way first." Tyler leaned over and brushed a lock of Phil's hair from his forehead. "This still feels so surreal. We're going to be seeing all these bands we love perform in person."

"I intend to soak in *all* this ambience and good music." Owen took another chug of water.

"We need to make sure we get a good view of the stage for the F-Holes, too." Jared reminded him. They were playing later Friday night.

"Yeah." Owen grinned. "I can't wait to hear Luka and

Dmitri play their cellos." He'd already handed his notice in at Arpeggios so that he and Jared could take some time off before his hectic rehearsal schedule and new role with Oriolidae started.

Lindsey had seen them off at the airport, sad she wasn't able to come with them. Since their heart-to-heart, her and Owen's relationship had felt more on an even keel. He had no idea how his parents' conversation had gone, but they were both going out of their way to be more involved in his life.

He and Lindsey still had a few arguments along the way, but that was to be expected, considering the years' of not-so-great vibes between them. Owen felt guilty about some of the narrative and assumptions he'd made to explain his mother's previous behaviour, but as Jared had pointed out, he'd done what he needed for his own peace of mind and had been quick to embrace his mother with open arms now she was trying to put things right.

Brett pulled up and parked the bus in the area put aside for performers. "This is us." He had family coming to the festival, so had planned to stay with them in their tent. "I'll be back on Sunday. Have fun. It's been great getting to know you. I'll be cheering loudly from the audience, but I know you're going to rock." He gave them each a grin. "Go Flightless!"

"Go Flightless!" they echoed.

"Such a nice guy," Rachel said. "We totally scored finding him." She got up from her seat and grabbed her large handbag, which rumour said was even bigger on the inside. "I'm going to go talk shop with a few people. Settle in and wander around. We'll meet up here later."

"Do you need a hand putting up the awning?" Owen asked Clay, who had offered to set up what would be their home away from home for the next few days. While the bus was roomy, with seats folding down into beds, they'd also hired a tent to attach to the side of it to give Rachel and Kaci some privacy.

"You're too late, mate." Phil grinned and wrapped his arm around Tyler's shoulders. "We've already got it all sussed. I've spent hours going over the instructions."

"More like a full ten minutes," Tyler corrected him good-naturedly, with a kiss. He wriggled his finger, which now sported a ring that matched Phil's. "Besides, this is good practice for all the organising we need to do for our wedding."

Jared groaned and then coughed. "Don't you already have that all under control? Or, at least, Phil's mum does, from what you've said."

"Ah, but we're only doing this once, so it has to be right." Tyler was determined that their wedding ceremony would be nothing less than perfection.

"Awww, but marrying you is everything I need, babe." Phil silenced Tyler with a kiss and waved at them with his free hand.

"I think they want some privacy," Clay announced. "Come on, Kaci. Plenty of time to worry about setting up. I could do with stretching my legs."

"We'll be back in an hour," Kaci said loudly.

"I'm not sure they heard you." Owen laughed.

Phil's silent two-fingered response left them all laughing.

"Clay and I will go find the water tent, or whatever it's called," Kaci offered. "You two can figure out the lay of the land, and we can report back here and interrupt the sweet but horny lovers in there."

"They'll calm down by Christmas." Jared followed Owen out of the van and pulled him into an embrace after their friends had walked away. "And attending a late December wedding will be the perfect way to round out the year."

"Yeah." Owen kissed Jared slow and deep. "I still can't believe this is our life. This time last year, things were very different."

"I prefer this over last year." Jared rested their foreheads together. "I'd given up finding a band where I fit, and now I have all that and you." He smiled. "I love you, sweetheart."

"Love you, too." Owen stretched his stiff shoulders. "Do you think we've done the right thing, not including anything new in this concert?"

He and Jared had almost finished the song they'd started at Frays on the beach that evening but decided to put it to one side until after Rocktoberfest.

"Yeah." Jared gestured for Owen to turn around and started massaging his shoulders. "Each time we play something new, I tense up, hoping the audience doesn't hate it."

"They always love our songs."

"This isn't our usual audience, though, and I'm not sure a love ballad is the right song for this." Jared kissed Owen's neck when he was done. "Walk and talk for a while?"

"Yeah, of course." Owen slipped his hand into Jared's and shrugged. "I think we have a good mix of rock and a couple of more melodic songs for this performance, though." He sighed.

"Penny for them?" Jared frowned. He always picked up on Owen's change of mood.

"What if this is our only chance for the spotlight?" Owen voiced the thoughts that had been growing since their arrival in the States. "We're a little drop in a huge lake. I'd love to think that this will be enough to propel us into rock stardom, but this is a four-day festival with heaps of fantastic bands, many of them who have already achieved that."

"You're worried that no one will be interested in an emerging band from small town New Zealand?"

"Something like that." Owen felt foolish mentioning it. "I haven't said anything because I don't want to bring anyone down." He hastily added, "but I know I can talk to you about this stuff."

"Good. I want you to be able to." Jared caressed Owen's thumb while they walked along. "And it's occurred to me too. I bet we're not the only ones." He stopped walking and turned to face Owen. "Do you know what I think? If we make it big, that's a bonus. We do this, we enjoy it, and if that's as far as we go, then that's okay." He shrugged. "We all have day jobs and if push comes to shove, we'll keep playing the pub circuit. We'll have this once-in-a-lifetime experience we can tell our kids about, as well as all the memories that go with it."

"And that will be enough, right?" Owen felt warm inside when Jared mentioned kids, although they'd never discussed their long-term future.

With the whirlwind of everything going on, they'd been focused on one day-at-a-time, one-gig-at-a-time, and getting here.

"I think so." Jared frowned. "Shit, I didn't mean anything by the kids comment. I don't want you to—"

"Think that was what you wanted." Owen smiled. "It's okay if you do. I love you. I meant what I said about wanting a future together." Since that day at Gran's, their path forward was clearer, but they'd never had time to sit down and figure out the day-to-day details and practical side of what that would look like.

"That's all I want too, sweetheart." Jared traced his fingers around the outline of Owen's smile. "As long as you're in my life, we'll make it work. The details will come later when we need them to."

~

"Shit, it's hotter than I thought it would be." Jared stared up at the cloudless sky. "I'm going to grab our water bottles before we go any further."

"Sounds like a plan." Owen grinned. "Don't tell Rachel we wandered off without them, or we'll never hear the end of it."

"We haven't gone far," Jared reminded him. "Barely out of earshot of the noise, I'll pretend I don't hear when I sneak in to grab them."

Owen laughed. "I'm sure Phil and Tyler will be too absorbed with each other to notice." He frowned, sure he could hear the unmistakable sounds of a cello. "I'm going to follow that music. See you in a few."

"As long as you don't find a trail of rats."

"Ha… ha. Wrong instrument." Owen rolled his eyes, listened again and headed in the direction of the cellist.

A dark-haired man sat in the shade of a bus, scowling as he played dissonant chords and contrapuntal melody on his cello.

Wow. Owen slowed to a halt when he realised who he was listening to, not sure he should be eavesdropping on an obvious attempt to exorcise demons with music.

He knew that look and how short-lived the result would be once he stopped playing. He'd attempted to forget his own issues that way too many times.

The cellist dragged out the final note, sighed, and closed his eyes. Despite the unhappy vibe coming off him in waves, he seemed less angry.

Or had buried it more successfully than before he'd started playing.

Owen couldn't help but clap. "Wow, love your Shostakovich."

"Wait…" The cellist looked startled. "You recognised that?"

"Well, yeah, his second concerto isn't exactly obscure." Owen hesitated. "I didn't realise you played classical, too." He stopped, suddenly second-guessing himself about the identity of the man in front of him. "You are Luka, right? From the F-Holes." He'd already made an idiot of himself. Why not go for broke? "I love you guys."

"Thanks. Yeah, I'm Luka. And until you said something, I would have thought Dmitri and I were the only two people here who'd recognise it. You're in one of the other bands?"

"Yeah, umm, hi." Owen breathed out a sigh of relief that he hadn't been mistaken. "I'm Owen. I play fiddle with Flightless."

"Oh? Sorry, I'm not familiar." Luka tilted his head to one side. "Not American, I take it? Though I can't place your accent."

"No worries." Owen shrugged, half expecting Luka's response. "I'd be surprised if you have heard of us. We're a Kiwi band…" He elaborated before Luka could make a comment about fruit or small native birds. "New Zealand, hence the accent." He laughed, still nervous about talking with someone way more successful than he'd probably ever be. "World famous in New Zealand… and probably only just." He fingered his cross. "Sorry, local joke." *Shit, way to go, Owen, referring to a local advert unfamiliar to anyone outside the country.* "Umm, not placing your accent either."

"Famous anywhere is better than nothing." Luka's lips twisted into a strained smile. "At least that's what I tried to tell my parents." He waved his hand dismissively. "My family is from Macedonia, but we came here when I was a kid."

"This is my first time out of New Zealand." Owen shrugged, attempting to appear nonchalant but certain he'd failed. Luka's comment about his parents hit a little too close to home. "And my mum's only just coming around to accepting what I do. She's spent years trying to convince me that I needed to get the band out of my system and pursue a real career in music."

"Shit, really?" Luka gaped at him. "Me too! Only my parents never accepted what I prefer to play or anything else about me. Shostakovich was only barely acceptable to them." He scowled. "Too modern."

"That sucks, and I like Shostakovich. Their loss." Owen lowered his voice, hoping he wasn't crossing a line with his next comment but sensing he might have found someone who agreed with it. "Though I must admit I'm not so fussed on some modern composers." He mock shuddered. "Too much mucking around with key and time signatures."

"I don't either." Luka shook his head. "But the folks were horrified I would rather shred my bow on Rammstein than Rimsky-Korsakov." He rolled his eyes. "They told me I'm wasting my education."

Owen snorted. "Yeah, and then it's followed by the reminder of how they've supported me to get that education, and had such high hopes for my future." He echoed Luka's eye roll. "My brother did the 'right thing' and plays flute with an orchestra. Worse when there's a comparison right there. My parents said all the right words when we'd had a gig, then I'd wait for the but…."

"*Exactly.*" Luka waved his bow in the air. "Only with mine, it was *my* damned scholarship that paid my way. But when your grandfather was in the USSR Symphony Orchestra, you've supposed to 'aspire higher than the low brow cretins around you.'"

"Ouch." Owen winced, then grew silent, torn between wanting to give Luka a hug and suspecting it wouldn't be appreciated. In the end, he spoke slowly, settling on sharing something he hoped would help. "I found out recently that

Mum wanted a career as a violinist, but it didn't work out, so she was determined that I should have what she lost." He couldn't stop the sigh that escaped his lips. His attempt to put that part of his past behind him was obviously not working as well as he'd thought. "I spent a lot of years knowing she wanted the best for me and trying to pull myself in two directions." He held up his hand in case Luka got the wrong idea. Fuck, he'd overshared more than he'd planned and didn't want to turn the conversation into a sob story about his own issues. "I'm not saying that's what you're going through. But yeah, family expectations get you with the guilt because deep down, there's always that thing that they love you and have the best of intentions."

"Intentions?" Luka laughed bitterly. "I could almost understand if one of my parents had a dream they couldn't fulfil and wanted to help me fulfil mine. My folks didn't have a musical bone in either of their bodies. So it was all about me being the only child and 'carrying on the Petrov legacy.' Not only did I want to play Metal, I wasn't about to marry and give them the grandchildren they so desperately want, so…" He shrugged. "You're lucky your folks love you. Mine only loved me when they thought I was what they want me to be."

"Oh fuck, I'm sorry." Owen's issues with his mum felt like nothing compared to the crap Luka was going through. "My parents didn't have an issue with me being bi, once they got what it meant." He chewed his lip. "That's one hell of a lot of unreasonable expectations. At some point, you've got to live your life for you." Yeah, and he'd done that so well before he'd met Jared. "Easier said than done, though. Your dreams, not theirs." He regretted his words as soon as he'd spoken. "And you sure as hell don't need me saying all that either. Sorry."

Luka ran a hand through his hair. "No, look, I'm sorry.

You're fine. You didn't need me dumping that on you. It's been kind of a shit day, and I get in a mood when I feel like I have no control over anything."

"You're not dumping on me, and it's fine." Owen wished he could do something to help and hoped he hadn't made Luka's mood worse by rambling on. "I escape into music when I get like that. It helps." He gestured to Luka's cello. "Guessing that's what the Shostakovich was. I find Beethoven good for that."

To his relief, Luka chuckled. "Yeah, or some Metallica. You should bring your 'fiddle' over sometime this weekend, we could totally thrill the unwashed masses with some of the Ariel Quartet. I could even get Dmitri to play violin. He's a switch in more ways than one."

"Seriously?" Owen stared at him, open-mouthed. "That would be amazing. I had no idea Dmitri plays violin as well." A thought occurred to him, and he admitted it sheepishly. "You know what's crazy? When I play with the band, I think of my violin as a fiddle. When I play classical, it's a violin. I really need to get over that."

"Yes, I'm serious," Luka confirmed. "And Dmitri will deign to use a 'tiny cello' on occasion. As long you don't go making bets with any hillbillies with your instrument, call it whatever you'd like."

Owen chuckled. "Not really any hillbillies around our way, so I think I'm safe." He turned at the sound of footsteps behind him. "Hey."

"Hey." Jared kissed Owen's cheek. He'd taken longer collecting their water bottles than he needed. Had he seen Owen and Luka talking and given them some time to connect? "Wondered where you got to. Everything okay?"

"Yeah. Luka, this is my boyfriend, Jared. Jared, Luka."

"Nice to meet you." Jared slipped his arm around Owen's waist. "Love your band, and looking forward to you playing."

He'd already figured out who Luka was, but then how many cellists would there be at Rocktoberfest?

Luka raised an eyebrow. "Thanks. Nice to meet you as well. We go on tomorrow night. When are you up?"

"Tomorrow afternoon," Owen said. "Slot before Grindstone." Already, their trip was bordering on surreal. Chatting with Luka from the F-Holes, on top of playing before Grindstone, made it an experience he wasn't about to forget.

"Hopefully, I'll get a chance to see you perform." Luka stood. "I should get back on the bus. They'll probably come looking for me soon. Later!"

"Later!" Owen watched Luka pick up his cello and led Jared away. "Such a nice guy," he said once they were out of earshot. "He's invited me to play with him and Dmitri sometime this weekend."

Jared's grip tightened around Owen's waist. "Sounds like fun. I'd love to listen." He paused and glanced back at the bus. "If that's okay, of course."

"Yeah, why wouldn't it be?" Owen frowned, and the penny dropped. "We chatted about music and other stuff. No flirting, I promise." He shrugged. No way would Luka be interested in him. "And besides, I'm taken. Very taken."

"Definitely." Jared scowled, then sighed. "Sorry. He's a good-looking guy, and whatever you were talking about seemed... intense." He looked sheepish. "Guess I overreacted and kind of staked my claim a bit."

"Really?" Owen gestured to a space between two vans, turned in Jared's arms, and kissed him fiercely. "You're mine, and while you doing that is hot, there's no need for it."

He leaned his forehead against Jared's, both of them breathing heavily.

"Yeah, sorry." Jared sounded sheepish. "Acted without thinking. Not usually my thing."

"Yeah, I know, and it's fine." Owen glanced at his watch,

surprised at how long he and Luka had chatted. "I figure Tyler and Phil have had their time." He nibbled on Jared's ear. "Want me to remind you we belong together?" He licked down Jared's neck.

Fuck, that groan was sexy as hell.

"Fuck, yeah." Jared's voice was hoarse. "Let's go make some music of our own."

CHAPTER SEVENTEEN

Don't look at the crowd. Don't look at the crowd. Jared glanced up, in spite of his determination not to, and his stomach churned.

Fuck, so many people. He fought the urge to run and wiped his hands on his black jeans.

Owen took a step back to briefly stand next to Jared. "You can do this, sweetheart. Focus on the music, not the crowd," he whispered.

Jared managed a shaky smile and thumbs up. He reached for his water bottle and took a few sips to steady his nerves.

"Hello, Rocktoberfest!" Clay addressed the crowd, looking as relaxed as he did when they played the small pub scene.

How the hell does he do it?

"It's an honour to play here for you today." Clay indicated the rest of the band and grinned. "We're Flightless, and here from New Zealand. This isn't only our first time at Rocktoberfest, but for most of us, our introduction to your lovely country too."

The crowd applauded.

"But enough from me. On with the music!" Clay turned to Kaci for her to lead them into their first song, *Sorted*.

Owen's violin sung above the other instruments. His eyes glazed over, lost in the music, the cross around his neck catching the stage lights.

Jared couldn't take his eyes off him. Shit, he was hot. Jared smiled, wondering, not for the first time, at how lucky he was.

Not only to be playing for this band but also to be with Owen. Whatever happened next, no one could take this moment from him.

The final notes of the song were greeted by applause. Someone yelled from the audience, "Go Flightless," and the call rippled through the audience.

Once they quietened, Owen played a lone note on his violin and began to sing the opening lines of *Patterns in the Sand*.

"Tiny grains of sand reflecting the patterns in my heart. Changing, lonely, needing more."

The ballad was followed by *Lost*, their decision to go for a mix of upbeat and slower songs paying off, given the rapt attention of their audience. The songs he and Owen had written to highlight the band members gave them each their moment to shine, and by the time the audience started singing along with the chorus to *Off Beat*, Jared started to relax and enjoy the experience.

Clay took a moment to introduce the band. "Thanks for being such an enthusiastic audience. I'm sure you want to know who you're listening to. I'm Clay. I'm mostly lead vocals, and while I do pick up a guitar from time to time, you'll be relieved that our resident guitarist, Phil, is way better than I am."

A few people in the audience laughed.

"Tyler's on bass," Clay continued, "and you can thank

Owen, our amazing fiddle player, and Jared on keyboards for the songs we're playing tonight."

Without further ado, Phil and Tyler launched into their song *Bass of My Heart*, and then Jared and Owen sang *Sunshine*.

The audience grew quiet after that performance. Jared hoped it was because they loved it, but their time was almost up.

Owen stepped up to the microphone. "Our last song holds a special place in my heart," he said, glancing at Jared and holding his gaze. "*Divided Road* was the first song Jared and I wrote together, and it reflected a time in my life when I thought I'd have to choose between two things I loved." He smiled. "Luckily, I found out I could have both, but anyway, here's *Divided Road*, and thanks for listening."

Jared took a deep breath. Although he'd already sung solo and with Owen, this song was important to him, too. Clay picked up his guitar and gave Owen a nod.

"Looking in the mirror, not loving what I see." Owen's voice sounded way more emotional than usual, but he didn't miss a beat.

After the shared bridge with Jared on keyboard, Owen walked over to him like it was only them on stage. "Not loving what I see. Not loving me."

Jared stopped playing, stood, and held out his hand to Owen. "I hold out my hand."

Owen's hand felt firm in Jared's, warm and loving, a reflection of Owen himself. "You pull me back to myself, to us, and what could be."

Jared kissed Owen's hand without thinking. Owen placed his violin on Jared's keyboard, and they took the next few steps together, Owen's arm around Jared's waist, an almost dance, singing in harmony, and then as one when they reached the end of the song.

"My divided road, now one."

~

Owen took a bow with the rest of the band, his heart pounding. He hadn't expected Jared's addition to their song, but it felt right, and he'd gone with the flow.

The audience whistled and applauded, showing their appreciation of the performance. Owen grinned, and the band all raised their arms together, separated long enough to grab their instruments and exit the stage.

"Wow." Kaci vocalised what Owen was thinking. "That was such a buzz."

"Well done!" Rachel was beaming. "You guys outdid your-selves." She turned to Jared. "That move, kissing Owen's hand, was inspired. I saw some of the audience reaching for tissues."

Jared blushed. "I didn't… it just happened, then…." He took a chug of water. "Fuck. I got caught up in the moment and thought I'd ruined everything."

"It was perfect, sweetheart." Owen kissed Jared's cheek.

"Totally." Phil clapped Jared on the back. "It added to the song and gave the lyrics even more heart and authenticity."

"Not that it didn't have any to start with," Tyler added.

"Yeah, that." Phil rolled his eyes.

"Come on, we need to clear the area for the next band." Rachel led them off the stage. "Go unwind and enjoy the rest of the music." Her phone buzzed with a message, and she retrieved it out of her bag. "I need to get this. Meet you at the bus later tonight?"

"Sure." Clay waited until she'd gone. "She got some news this morning that got her way excited, but she wouldn't say what it was."

"Maybe that's what she wants to talk to us about tonight?" Owen suggested.

"I'm going to be too buzzed to sleep," Kaci announced.

On stage, the stagehands were setting up for the next act. Axel from Grindstone paused as his band passed theirs. "Great performance. Loved it!"

"Thanks." Owen's mouth felt dry at the unexpected compliment. "Good luck with your performance. Though I doubt you need it. Love your music."

Axel's grin was more than thanks enough.

Owen stared after him. This festival was definitely one for meeting his favourite bands. Jared's stomach growling yanked him back to reality. "We need to grab some food before we settle in to watch. Someone hasn't eaten much today."

"Neither have you!" Jared protested.

"Yeah, but at least I'm not obvious about it." Owen had been too psyched up to eat, anything apart from a muesli bar first thing, although he'd made sure they'd both drunk enough to get through the performance. He threaded his free hand through Jared's. "I'm going to pack my violin away, and then we'll eat and enjoy the rest of the music, yeah?"

"I'll save you guys a spot so you don't miss Grindstone," Kaci offered.

"Thanks," Owen said. They didn't have far to go to the secure space, and he'd left a bag there with snacks.

Jared pulled him in for a kiss immediately after they reached a semi-private corner. The festival-goers didn't seem to be fussed about PDAs, although a few had smiled seeing them obviously together.

"That was one hell of a performance," he whispered when they broke the kiss. "Thanks for getting me through that, sweetheart."

"You got through it yourself," Owen told him. "You were

amazing." He'd felt tears well when they'd sung that last song together.

"You bring out the best in me." Jared kissed him again, this time on the cheek. "And that was so a prelude for tonight's symphony."

Owen laughed. He'd never get tired of using that description. When he and Jared made love, it was the best kind of music.

"We'll have a full bus and more." He placed a finger across Jared's lips. "But I can be quiet if you can."

"Challenge accepted." Jared's grin widened. "You're on." He threaded his fingers through Owen's and followed him to the secure space.

Applause echoed through the crowd. Grindstone must be already on stage. Owen stowed his violin and grabbed their snacks. Hopefully, Kaci had found them a good spot. He didn't want to miss any of the performance.

"Hello, Rocktoberfest!" Axel yelled to the crowd.

"Hey, Canadian," someone in the audience shouted back.

Big Mac strummed a chord on his bass, and the band began their first song.

"Haven't heard this one before." Jared's expression brightened with excitement. "Come on, we don't want to miss it!"

The crowd was huge. Owen looked around for Kaci, but couldn't see her anywhere. He hoped she managed to get a good spot, but they were on their own trying to snag one.

The sun was beginning to set, bathing their surroundings in an almost ethereal glow, but thankfully taking its time heading into darkness so there was still plenty of light to see by.

He and Jared made their way through the crowd, edging through any gaps they could find with murmured apologies. Most of the audience were too engrossed in the performance to notice them.

"There are a couple of spots up the front," Jared said.

"Should we? We're late, and someone...." Owen stopped mid-sentence. They would have grabbed those if they hadn't been on stage, and they *were* up for grabs. And this was *Grindstone*.

On stage, Ed was talking, introducing a young woman from their old high school who was singing for them.

Wow. Owen had to remember their mission for a good view of the stage once Marley started singing.

"Brilliant, wow." Jared voiced Owen's thoughts and echoed the murmurs of the people around them. "Quick, that gap over there while everyone's distracted."

They ducked through, applause loud around them, almost at the front when Axel started singing another new song.

Owen grinned. *In Another Life* was so obviously a love song, and Axel had totally fallen for the lucky guy it was for.

Shit, everyone was looking where they were headed.

Axel scanned the audience, pressed his fingers to his lips, winked, and then grabbed his mic again. "Yes, we're going to rock your world."

"I've seen him before," Jared whispered, gesturing to the guy in the audience in front of them.

"You're the teacher." A woman to their left obviously recognised him, too. She gave him a huge hug, and he leaned into the embrace.

Owen followed Jared's gaze. "Shit, you're right. You're both right." He'd seen photos. Now they were closer, there was no mistaking the red hair and build of Hugo, Axel's teacher.

He edged nearer and lost his footing, accidentally jostling Hugo in the process.

"Oh, sorry." Hugo apologised.

"No, my bad," Owen said quickly.

Hugo turned. "Owen?"

Shit, he knows who I am. Owen felt a moment's confusion. Duh, of course, Hugo would recognise him. Flightless had just been on stage, and Clay had introduced each of them. "Sorry, still getting used to being recognised." He grinned. "Yeah. We've snuck down here because we're huge fans of Grindstone," he added quickly.

Jared squeezed his hand, his expression matching Owen's. "What better way to enjoy the show." At least he had his wits about him to make it sound like they were being smooth about it rather than slipping through the crowd to get a decent spot.

"You guys..." Hugo spoke slowly like he was searching for the right words. "That kind of talent." Thankfully he kept his voice low so they wouldn't attract attention.

"Hugo, right?" Owen figured he'd better confirm Hugo's identity before he spoke further. "You were Axel's teacher?"

"We weren't involved." Hugo flushed.

"We've read the stories." Owen waved his hand to show they weren't bothered by, or believed them. "So, you're Canadian?" he asked to lighten the tension, although he recognised the accent.

Hugo smiled. "Yes. Very Canadian."

"And you also taught Marley? Wow." Owen had always admired Hugo and how he'd helped musicians reach their potential.

"Yeah, Marley's my student."

"We heard her as we were coming down. She's seriously talented."

"She is."

"Do you think she'll be playing with them regularly?" Jared asked.

"I honestly don't know," Hugo answered. "If the song went over well with the crowd tonight, I do know they might put it on the next studio album."

"We already own all their albums." Owen nudged Jared. Their music collections were similar. Perhaps going forward, they'd only need to buy one of anything new between them. "But we're going to have to buy their next one when it comes out." He smiled at Jared and swallowed, the thought of them as a couple never failing to make his heart soar.

"The band will appreciate the sale."

"We're hoping we might run into them at some point this week. We've only been able to exchange a few words."

"I'm sure they'd love that," Hugo said, his confident tone a reminder of his history with the band. "They're... really down to earth."

"And Axel's in love." Owen doubted Axel's focus on this particular section of the audience wasn't a coincidence. "If that new song was any indication."

Hugo's blush was sweet and suggested he'd been the one Axel had sought out in the crowd. Owen hoped things worked out for them. He turned to Jared, unsure how to break off the conversation without being rude while giving Hugo some space.

Luckily, the next song ended, and the cheers from the audience provided the distraction he needed. Owen leaned into Jared. They shared a brief kiss and focused on enjoying the rest of the performance.

～

"Reality is going to be kind of a letdown after the last few days." Jared eyed up the bus and checked around it and under it. He was sure he'd forgotten something and would remember what it was once they were several hours down the road.

"Rocktoberfest was even more amazing than I thought it would be." Owen drank deeply from his water bottle and then wiped his mouth. "I still can't believe I got to play with Luka and Dmitri, and we spent some time with Grindstone." He mocked sighed. "My life is complete."

Jared rolled his eyes. "Wow, thanks." He laughed, knowing Owen would take the comment with the humour it was meant. "I enjoyed that too," he added softly. "All of it." Everyone they'd met had been friendly and... for all their fame, acted no differently for it. "Being able to come together and share our passion for music was amazing. Even if this is our one and only Rocktoberfest, I'm never going to forget it."

"Not going to miss this heat, though."

"At least we're going back into spring and not winter." Jared was tempted to lick the droplets of water from the crease in Owen's smile, but not in company, which would give their friends way too much teasing fodder.

Not that it would take much. The band's mutual good-humoured banter reminded Jared of his relationship with Brigit and made him smile, although he'd never admit that to any of them.

"Yeah, there's that." Jared glanced around once more and then shrugged. Whatever he'd forgotten would have to stay here, lost forever to the desert. "I guess I don't really want to leave, although I do miss home."

"Yeah, me too, although I bet Bach is being spoilt rotten." Owen snuck a quick kiss. "I'm looking forward to some privacy, too. You'll stay over for a few days, yeah?"

"I'd love to."

Before they'd left for the States, Jared had spent more nights at Owen's than at home. The lease was up on Jared's flat in another six months, and as much as he was tempted to move in with Owen and put what he paid in rent towards Owen's mortgage, it wasn't his house or his call.

Owen had enough changes in his life with quitting Arpeggios and starting with Oriolidae. Staying over was way different than living together full-time. Their relationship was already moving faster than either of them had expected, and Jared was content to wait to take the next step when the time was right, and both of them were ready.

"There she is!" Kaci ran down the steps of the bus. "Do you know who that is with her?" She shaded her eyes against the sun and waved at Rachel.

Clay, Phil, and Tyler joined them.

"You don't know?" Clay asked.

The two men were dressed semi-casually in shorts and button-down shirts. Jared frowned. "They were chatting with Rachel the other night."

"She never told me what their conversation was about, just that patience is a virtue." Kaci pouted. "It totally isn't, by the way, and she needs to practice what she preaches."

"Way too much info, Kaci." Clay grinned.

"Yeah, whatever." Kaci poked her tongue at him.

"Children, behave," Tyler teased.

"And that goes for the peanut gallery, too," Owen added, although they all grew silent when Rachel and her companions came close enough to overhear.

Whatever Rachel had been going to tell them a few nights ago hadn't eventuated. They'd all been hyped and tired, and all she'd say was that she was waiting until everything was in place first.

Looked like that might be now.

Rachel introduced them. "Derek and Neil, this is Flightless. Clay, Owen, Kaci, Jared, Phil, and Tyler. Guys, this is Derek Addington and Neil Latkey."

"Pleasure to finally meet you." Derek was softly spoken, with red hair and a warm smile. "Neil and I loved your performances, both here and at Frays, a few months ago."

"We already had tickets for Rocktoberfest and were thrilled that you were going to be performing here." Neil was a fraction shorter than Derek, and the closeness in which they stood together suggested they were either together or very good friends. They both spoke with Kiwi accents, and their names sounded familiar, but Jared couldn't place them.

"You've been in Arpeggios," Owen said slowly. "A few times, but not so much the last year or so."

"We used to work in Upper Hutt," Neil explained, "but then we moved into Wellington when an opportunity came up to expand our business, but we kept the name as a nod to our original premises."

The penny dropped. Jared glanced at Neil and Derek and then at Rachel. "Shit…" he blurted. "Sorry, I've just realised who you are. You've come into the Scone a few times when I've worked there. My sister was way excited when you made it big."

"We're more well known by our business name." Neil paused before continuing. "Keats Street Studio."

Rachel grinned, her professional demeanour suddenly giving way to excitement. "They want to take you on as clients and produce your songs."

"An album with Keats Street Studio?" Clay looked stunned. "Oh my God. I've been following your label since you started up in your home studio. I should have realised who you are immediately."

"No worries, and we tend to keep our identities out of the public arena as much as possible." Neil smiled at Derek. "It's a luxury that, unfortunately, most bands don't have, being more in the public eye."

"I've read through the contract, and it's very comprehensive and generous," Rachel assured them, "but of course, this needs to be your decision."

"We've been watching you for a while, but with your change of lineup and rumours that Owen could be leaving, we wanted to see you perform a few more times and get a feel for the new songs you've been playing." Derek continued the conversation. "And, of course, confirm that the band we saw would be the same one we signed up."

"Our current lineup isn't changing," Owen reassured them, "and I'm not leaving. I will be playing with Oriolidae, but they've assured me they're happy for me to continue with Flightless, too."

"I'm already in talks with the quartet to make sure our schedules can accommodate performances and recording, so that won't be a problem," Rachel said.

"Fantastic," Neil said. "We'll be in touch once we're all back in Wellington, then, with your answer. That will give you time to get past the Rocktoberfest buzz and over the jetlag." He glanced at Tyler and Phil, who were holding hands. "And I assure you my husband and I don't tolerate any hate speech of any kind. We pride ourselves on being inclusive and supportive. As far as we're concerned, anyone working with us is family."

"We'll be in touch very soon," Rachel promised. "And I know I speak for all of us in saying we're thrilled and excited at the opportunity to work with you."

"As are we." Neil grinned. "Later, gentlemen and ladies."

"Shit, we're totally in," Kaci said after they walked away. "Aren't we?" She caught Rachel's eyes and quickly added, "after reading the contract first, of course."

"Totally." Phil shoulder-bumped Tyler and then kissed him. "Our future's looking golden, babe."

"Yep." Tyler kissed Phil's cheek. "Lots of work, but way worth it. I wouldn't have it any other way."

"Shit yeah." Jared squeezed Owen's hand. "I still can't believe it."

"Wow." Owen leaned into Jared. "We'll read the contracts, of course, but I trust you, Rachel."

"What Owen said." Clay grinned from ear to ear. "Fuck,

we've made it. I was prepared to go return to Wellington and back to what we've been doing. Hell, I thought that was what would happen."

"You've all deserved this," Rachel said. "You've worked hard, and when you play together, it's magic. I knew it was only a matter of time before someone noticed that." She grinned. "And I'm also pleased that I've taught you well, and you'll be reading the contract first before signing."

She gestured for them to huddle together into a group hug.

"Go Flightless!"

EPILOGUE

"And that's a wrap!" Hamish, the sound designer, gave them a thumbs up a few moments after the last note of their final song of their first album, *Divided Road*. "Sounds great. Well done, guys."

Owen grinned, hiding his exhaustion. The last few months had been a challenge, with recording at Keats Street and preparing for his first concert with the quartet the weekend before, but he'd made it. "I'm going to sleep for a week after this." He put away his violin and bow, and closed the case, determined to walk away from the instrument for a few days.

"You've deserved it, sweetheart." Jared kissed him soundly and wrapped his arm around Owen's waist. "We've all worked hard, and wow, what a buzz."

"I still can't believe we've recorded an album." Kaci did a celebratory roll on the drum, finishing with a tap of the cymbals. "Go us."

"Meeting in the green room." Rachel poked her head around the corner. "Lunch on Neil and Derek, and then the next couple of weeks are all yours."

Derek was waiting for them with a couple of bottles of champagne. "Congratulations on getting to the finish line. We appreciate all the hard work you've put in."

"Help yourself." Neil gestured to the huge spread. "I have a very good feeling about this album, especially considering the success of your first single."

Although they'd signed up with the studio for an album, Neil had decided to release their new song, *Sunset*, first to test the waters. The single had jumped up the New Zealand charts and sat on the number one spot for a week, performing way beyond any of the band's expectations.

Owen smiled softly at Jared. *Sunset* was the song they'd both vowed they'd write that evening they'd bared their souls on the beach at Napier. "I'm glad you talked us into releasing it now rather than keeping it for Frays later in the year."

"The song needed to be shared," Neil agreed. "It spoke to me, and I had a strong feeling it would to others, too."

"I learnt very early in our relationship that ignoring Neil's gut was a mistake." Derek grinned.

Neil elbowed him affectionally and grinned smugly. "Love you, too, Der." He cleared his throat. "So... I hope you've already started thinking about new songs for your next album. We don't want to wait too long between them. Strike while the iron is hot and all that."

"We have a few ideas," Owen admitted.

"And we're looking forward to the tour," Clay added. He and Nat had just announced their engagement, so they had a wedding to plan too.

Rachel had organised a New Zealand tour, with their last stop being in Wellington a few days before their album released. They were also doing a special stop at Frays as a thank you to Duncan for all his support and to catch up with Lincoln, who had moved up there until he figured out his future.

Beth's funeral a few months ago had been a celebration of her life. They'd dedicated their first album to her, an acknowledgement of the huge part she'd played in their lives, especially during the early days of the band.

"Phil and I are disappearing for a bit after this." Tyler popped a slice of ham into Phil's mouth. "With everything going on, we never got a proper honeymoon, so don't contact us while we're away because we *will* ignore you."

"Uh huh." Rachel's expression suggested the threat was an empty one.

"Owen and I are taking some time off too." Jared reminded her. He'd taken leave from the Scone, and Owen had two weeks off before Oriolidae rehearsals began again, although he'd already begun familiarising himself with the music.

"Some time for us and for the creative juices to start flowing again," Owen said, although he already had a few melodies needing lyrics, and Jared several lyrics that needed music.

Music was too much a part of their lives to walk away from, even temporarily, although he was determined they carve out some time together to relax without any interruptions.

Bach would be delighted to have Owen home for a while, although she'd dump him the instant Jared showed up. The two of them had bonded, with Bach having decided Jared's lap was far superior to Owen's for some reason.

Owen smiled. He was fond of sleeping with his head on Jared's lap, too, so he could see the appeal.

"Enjoy your break, everyone, and don't forget to make sure you put those plans into action." Neil stood. "We don't want you guys burning out. Music is fun, but it's also work."

"What he said." Derek led Neil out the door, the two of them disappearing towards their shared office.

"We totally made the right decision signing with them," Kaci said once they were out of earshot. "They have that balance between friendly and getting the job done."

Owen yawned. "Sorry, that wasn't about what you said. I'm tired." He hadn't drunk champagne in a while, either.

"I'll drop you home." Jared was on his feet in an instant. He'd offered to drive and spent the night before at Owen's.

"If you need us, call." Owen hoped the fresh air would give him a second wind. He had something to do before taking a way overdue nap. "But that's only a free pass until tomorrow evening." He gave Rachel a pointed look.

"Uh huh." She grinned and then winked at Kaci. "Text if you need me, and then I can decide whether it's urgent or can wait. We're taking the next few days off too."

"And so you should." Owen suspected she and Kaci might be announcing something soon, given how much time they spent together. They made a cute couple, Kaci was happy, and both Owen and Clay agreed she and Rachel were good for each other.

Kaci had often reminded them that she didn't need a couple of pseudo-brothers. Neither of them was giving up that role anytime soon.

～

"You look tired," Jared said when they pulled up outside Owen's. "You've been way busy the last month. I've been worried about you."

"I *am* tired." Owen didn't bother disagreeing as Jared wouldn't believe him. "I'd love some tea when we get home, and then…."

"Sure." Jared bit his lip as though suddenly nervous. "Do you want me to stay? You're tired and…."

"About that." Owen regretted the words when Jared

flinched. "God, no, not what you're probably thinking. Come in. We need to talk."

"Sure." Jared repeated. He waited for Owen to get out of the car and followed him into the house, bending to pet Bach when she greeted him like she hadn't seen him for months.

"Come here, sweetheart." Owen pulled Jared into a hug. "I've been wanting to talk about this for weeks, but life has been crazy, and I didn't want this to sound like an afterthought." He kissed Jared fiercely, putting all his love into the gesture.

Jared leaned into the kiss, deepening it. When he broke it, he rested his forehead against Owen's. "I love you. With everything I am. Whatever happens, I don't regret our time together. Not one moment of it."

"I love you too." Owen brushed Jared's hair off his forehead, loving the softness of it under his fingertip. "Move in with me."

Jared pulled back, shock over his face. "That's what you wanted to say? I thought…" He scrubbed at his face. "Shit, when you said you wanted to talk. Fuck, sorry, I'm tired, and… with all the time we were spending together, I thought you might need some space for a while."

"Is that a yes to moving in?" Owen had never doubted Jared's response. Until now. "I love you being around, and you're here more often than not anyway. I want you. I want us."

"It's a yes." Jared licked his lips, the nervousness back again. "Actually, there was something I wanted to talk to you about too, and then…" He looked embarrassed. "I still can't believe I doubted you wanted me here. Not after everything we've been to each other."

"You can talk to me about anything, sweetheart." Owen would make sure they both found time to catch up on sleep. "And never doubt I want you because that will never change."

"This isn't how I wanted to do this. I was planning for a few days time and to find somewhere romantic, but I've changed my mind." Jared got down on one knee.

Owen swallowed. *God, did this mean what he thought it did?*

"Marry me, Owen." Jared pulled a black case from his pocket, and opened it to reveal a slender gold ring. "I love you, and I can't imagine my life without you. I don't want to. Please say yes."

"Yes, yes, yes!" Owen's heart sped up. He held out his hand.

The ring was engraved on the inside with musical notes and two hearts intertwined, and fit perfectly on his finger like it was meant to be there.

He held his hand up, the sun reflecting off the gold. A melody came to his mind unbidden, and he grinned.

"You know," he said. "Our first song together was about a divided road, but I think we've been travelling the same one since we met. Again." He paused. "Beer Guy."

Jared chuckled. "*Your* Beer Guy."

"Hold that thought." Owen ran to the bedroom and grabbed something hidden in a sock in his bottom drawer. When he re-entered the living room, he held out an identical black case. "Asking you to move in was part one."

He got down on one knee. Jared had done this properly, so he would too. "I'll marry you, but only if you marry me too."

"I don't think that's…" Jared started to laugh. The sound was light, musical, and full of love. "Yes, definitely yes."

Owen slid the ring on Jared's finger. "The prelude to our symphony, sweetheart."

Jared replied in song, the familiar words now a part of both their hearts. "A love meant to be." He took Owen's hand, pulled him to his feet, and they danced a few steps together.

"Magic in song. I've chosen my future, made my decision,"

Owen sang softly, smiling when Jared joined in with a tweaked final line of what would forever be their song.

"*Our* divided road, now one."

ABOUT THE AUTHOR

CONNECT WITH ANNE
Contact me at:
annebarwell.wordpress.com
darthanne@gmail.com

~

Anne Barwell lives in Wellington, New Zealand. She shares her home with kitty siblings Byron and Marigold who are convinced her office chair is theirs.

In 2008, Anne completed her conjoint BA in English Literature and Music/Bachelor of Teaching. She has worked as a music teacher, a primary school teacher, and now works in a library. She is a member of the Upper Hutt Science Fiction Club and plays violin for Hutt Valley Orchestra.

She is an avid reader across a wide range of genres and a watcher of far too many TV series and movies, although it can be argued that there is no such thing as "too many." These, of course, are best enjoyed with a decent cup of tea and further the continuing argument that the concept of "spare time" is really just a myth. She also hosts and reviews for other authors, and writes monthly blog posts for Love Bytes. She is the co-founder of the New Zealand Rainbow Romance writers, and a member of RWNZ.

Anne's books have received honourable mentions five times, reached the finals four times—one of which was for best gay book—and been a runner up in the Rainbow Awards. She has also been nominated three times in the Goodreads M/M Romance Reader's Choice Awards—twice for Best Fantasy, once for Best Historical, and once for All-Time Favourite M/M Author.